The CAMPAIGN

LEILA SALES
ILLUSTRATED BY KIM BALACUIT

Amulet Books
New York

Library of Congress Cataloging-in-Publication Data

Names: Sales, Leila, author. | Balacuit, Kim, illustrator.
Title: The campaign / Leila Sales ; illustrations, Kim Balacuit.
Description: New York : Amulet Books, an imprint of Abrams, 2020. |
    Audience: Ages 8 to 12. | Summary: Twelve-year-old Maddie runs her
    babysitter Janet's campaign to become mayor of their city and protect
    arts funding.
Identifiers: LCCN 2019053253 | ISBN 9781419739743 (hardback) | ISBN
    9781419739750 (paperback) | ISBN 9781683357162 (ebook)
Subjects: CYAC: Political participation—Fiction. | Elections—Fiction. |
    Middle schools—Fiction. | Schools—Fiction.
Classification: LCC PZ7.S15215 Cam 2020 | DDC [Fic]—dc23
LC record available at https://lccn.loc.gov/2019053253

ABRAMS The Art of Books
195 Broadway, New York, NY 10007
abramsbooks.com

For Brian Pennington

CHAPTER 1

When I showed up for the first day of seventh grade, I'd already color-coded my schedule.

Gray was for periods that were definitely going to be miserable (math, science and technology, social studies, Spanish, health, homeroom, assembly).

Yellow was for periods that might be okay (English, PE).

Red was for periods that I was actually looking forward to (art, music, lunch).

School had barely begun, and already this year was looking like just one big expanse of gray.

Social studies was the first class of the day, and the teacher, Mr. Valdez, began by handing out blank paper and telling us to draw maps of the United States. "Don't stress over this. I don't expect you to know where every state is," he said.

Which was a relief, since I didn't know where *any* states were, and even though I was accustomed to failing to meet expectations, I'd hate to do so on the first assignment of the year.

"Just do your best for today," Mr. Valdez went on. "Put down whatever states you can remember, wherever you think they go. Trust me, by the end of the semester, you'll be able to draw this map with your eyes closed!"

Which is not true. I can't even draw my own face with my eyes closed, and I've been working on that for years. It always winds up with the nose and mouth on top of each other and the ears way off somewhere in space.

"Please take the next ten minutes to work on this," Mr. Valdez instructed.

I started out trying to follow the assignment to draw a faithful map of the country, but then I wound up going in sort of a different direction . . .

"Okay," Mr. Valdez said once our ten minutes were up, "now I'd like you to share your map with the student sitting next to you."

Naturally the student sitting next to me was My Friend Daniel, and naturally he just about died laughing when he looked at my map. Which would have been fine, because I knew what I'd done was kind of ridiculous, and I knew My Friend Daniel would appreciate it. But what *wasn't* fine was that he then tapped on the shoulder of Polly, the girl sitting in front of him, and said, "Hey, take a look at what Maddie drew. She thinks the state of Colorado is actually *shaped like* a mountain!"

"I do not," I objected. "I just thought it'd be more

interesting to draw a mountain than to draw a rectangle in the middle of the page and call it Colorado. I was capturing the essence of the state. Colorado's essence is mountainous."

Now Polly's two best friends, Molly and Holly, also turned around to look at my map.

"What?" giggled Molly. "Why didn't you just do the assignment, Maddie?"

Holly just gave me a look. Holly rarely says much—at least not loud enough for me to hear, though she's always whispering with her friends. Instead, she just communicates by looking sort of disgusted.

THE HOLLY LOOK

The three of them held up their maps, which all looked pretty much the same and pretty much like every other map of America that I'd ever seen.

"I was being *creative*, Molly and Polly and Holly," I told them wearily.

"Who are you calling Molly and Polly and Holly?" asked Polly.

"You three."

"But none of those is my name," said Molly. "My name is Adrianne."

"And my name is Dahlina," said Polly. "You know that."

I turned to the last girl and asked, "Do you have anything to add?"

"Not really," she said. "My name actually is Holly."

MOLLY/ADRIANNE   HOLLY/HOLLY   POLLY/DAHLINA

Same rhinestone headband

Same unicorn backpack

Same glittery pen that smears everywhere

Same ink stains from same glittery pen

Same boring accurate map of America

"You might as well all have rhyming names," I said, "since it seems like you want to be as similar to one another as possible."

Of course they're not *exactly* the same—for one thing, Holly is white, Polly is Indian, and Molly is black, plus they all have different body shapes and hair colors. But none of this stops them from acting like identical triplets or clones.

Molly rolled her eyes. "Why are you so weird?"

"Wasn't her map weird?" asked My Friend Daniel. "That's why I wanted to show it to you guys. I was like, whoa, Maddie's map is so *weird*, I bet they'd want to see how weird it is!"

"You are not helping, My Friend Daniel," I told him.

"See, even that is weird," commented Polly. "Why do you call him *My Friend Daniel*?"

"Because Daniel is his name," I answered, "and 'My Friend' is an honorific. You know, like how you'd say 'Prince William' instead of just 'William' or 'Captain Underpants' instead of just 'Underpants.' 'My Friend' is Daniel's title."

They stared at me.

"*You* don't have to call him My Friend Daniel," I reassured them. "He's not *your* friend."

"But I could be," Daniel interjected, still smiling. "I am fully ready to be Anybody's Friend Daniel!"

"Eyes to the front," Mr. Valdez said from his desk. "Time to start talking about America, folks."

The Three Meansketeers turned back around. I spent the rest of the period refusing to look at My Friend Daniel, except to occasionally glare at him.

"Do you think they want to be friends with me?" asked Daniel as the period ended and he watched Molly and Holly and Polly run for the door like a school of fish.

"Um," I said.

My Friend Daniel didn't wait for my reply. "They definitely seem to want to be friends with me," he said with a nod. "Definitely. I'm going to invite them to my bar mitzvah."

And somehow *I'm* the weird one?

CHAPTER 2

The best part of the first day of school finally came at 12:55 in the afternoon: art class!

"Hello, Mr. Xian!" I hollered as I ran into the art room. "Did you miss me?"

Mr. Xian laughed. He is the only teacher in school who actually likes me. "I certainly did," he replied. "Now, let me see what you've been working on."

That's what Mr. Xian says every time I see him. It makes me want to work on things just so I have something to show him.

"I finished two sketchbooks over the summer," I told him. "I brought them with me today so you could see.

I've been working on superheroes. So here's my Wonder Woman, and here's my Thor, and this is—"

"Batman," the art teacher said, holding up my sketchbook so he could inspect it. "I love how you've captured the sense of movement here."

"Thanks! And then I made up superheroes of my own. This one is you."

"I am very flattered," Mr. Xian said. "Though I'll have you know that I do *not* need a haircut. This is just how Art-Guys wear their hair. Now, for the next superhero you draw, I want you to play with angles. Do you think Art-Guy would seem more powerful if we were looking down on him or up at him?"

Mr. Xian simultaneously makes me feel like I've done good work and gives me ideas for doing even better. I don't know how he does it. When we do peer critiques, usually the other students just say, "It's good," which, while flattering, doesn't exactly help me improve. And I *want* to improve, because I want to be a professional cartoonist someday. Maybe I'll write graphic novels or work for Marvel or an animation studio. I'm a better artist than most twelve-year-olds, I think, but I still have a lot of work to do before I'm as good as Mr. Xian.

Once the rest of the class was seated, he started talking us through what we were going to be studying this semester. I doodled as he spoke, which is a thing I do that my fourth-grade teacher called "a bad habit." She said it made me look like I wasn't paying attention. I told her that I actually paid *better* attention if I was doodling at the same time. She didn't believe me.

Mr. Xian doesn't care if I doodle during class. He can tell I'm paying attention.

He told us about how we were going to do pottery this year, and for the first time all day, I finally relaxed. There aren't many places in school where I can do that. But even people who are mean to me, like Holly and Molly and Polly, leave me alone when we're in the art studio. I think it's because I never do anything dumb or weird during art, like making a map wrong or forgetting the multiplication tables or sounding out a word that I'm supposed to know already.

It's not really possible to do anything dumb or weird during art, because art doesn't have just one right answer.

I think that's what I like about it.

When class ended, I very slowly gathered up my materials and very slowly packed up my bag. I'm usually in a rush to get to the next place, but I never rush to leave the art room. It smells good, like paint and turpentine and freedom. I took a couple more deep breaths, trying to keep the smell with me for the rest of the day.

"Maddie," Mr. Xian said as I was zippering up my bag. I was the last student left in the room. "I want you to know . . . well, just that I hope you don't ever stop creating. You have a unique perspective. If you keep at it, you could be a truly top-notch artist someday."

This was, without question, the literal and absolute *best* thing that anybody had ever said to me.

I was so happy that I couldn't help but jump up and down a little. "Thank you so much!" I told him. "Of *course* I'll keep at it. Making art is my favorite thing in the world."

"Good," Mr. Xian said. "That's good. You need to remember that, Maddie, because you'll find that not everybody values art as highly as we do. Some people think it's a waste of time and money."

"They're wrong," I said.

He laughed. "Sure are." But he sounded sad.

"What idiots even think that?" I asked.

"Unfortunately, one of them is going to be the next mayor of Lawrenceville," he said.

"Blech." I made a face. "What's happening to our current mayor?"

"Mayor Peñate is retiring at the end of this term," Mr. Xian told me. "So in November there's going to be an election for a new mayor. But the election is basically all sewn up, because only one candidate is running. Her name's Lucinda Burghart."

"And she doesn't like art?" I said.

"I don't know her, so I can't say that she doesn't *like* it, but she certainly doesn't think it's very important. She's been on the city council for years now and is always putting forward bills to cut 'unnecessary' expenses—and she definitely puts art in that category. She's been very clear that once she becomes mayor, the first thing she's going to do is slash funding for arts education: visual arts, drama, music, all of it. Which means no more art supplies, no more art shows, no more museum field trips . . . and no more job for me."

Mr. Xian gave me a weak smile. "I'll be fine," he said. "As soon as I saw which way this election was going, I started putting out feelers for jobs teaching art in other cities. Or maybe I'll move to a private school where they have a budget for arts education. I'll find another job, Maddie—don't worry about me. It just won't be in any of this city's public schools."

"Okay . . ." I said. I believed Mr. Xian when he said he'd get a job someplace else, because he was a really good teacher and I bet lots of places would want to hire him. But it didn't seem fair. And anyway, he didn't—and maybe couldn't—answer my next question:

Without art, what was *I* going to do?

CHAPTER 3

"Janet!" I shouted as soon as I reached her car at the end of the school day. I threw my bag into the back seat, slammed the back door, threw myself into the front seat, and then slammed that door, too.

"What's up, Mads?" Janet asked.

Janet is twenty-three, and she used to babysit me when I was little and she was in high school. Then she went off to college, and I didn't see her for four years. Now she's back and she's taking care of me again, which is kind of stupid, because I am already as old as she was when she first started babysitting other people's kids. But I'm not complaining, because there are things Janet can do that I can't, like drive and cook. Plus she's basically paid to hang out with me, which is nice because most people won't hang out with me for free.

JANET, THE WORLD'S GREATEST SUPER-BABYSITTER!

Superpower is that everybody likes her!

Friendship bracelet that I made for her!

Can solve any problem!

Phone never leaves her side!

Tote bag carries a book, chocolate bars, and googly-eye stickers, because she's always prepared!

Toenails are painted aqua, except for this one which is her "party nail" and it's gold!

"It's going to rain tomorrow," Janet told me as she started up the car and began driving toward my house. "I can't *wait.*"

Janet is extremely into weather. It's her favorite hobby. She's the moderator of this amateur meteorology website, where she's always chatting with other weather fans about storm systems and air pressure and something called "isobars." She likes big, dramatic blizzards best, but she also loves a good sunny day, and she says that rain is beautiful and that even general cloud cover can be pretty interesting. I have never found a type of weather that Janet doesn't like, which means that whatever is going to happen tomorrow, she is always excited for it.

I think that seems like a nice way to live.

That day, though, I felt like there were things going on the world that were even more important than weather.

"Did you know that we're getting a new mayor this year?" I demanded. "Her name is Lucinda Burghart. And she's going to *get rid of art classes in schools.*"

Janet thought about this for a moment. "I knew Mayor Peñate was retiring," she said. "I haven't been paying much attention to who might take over after him. But hold on—Election Day isn't even until November. So there's no guarantee that she'll be the next mayor."

"Yes, there is." After talking to Mr. Xian, I'd looked up Lucinda Burghart in our local newspaper, the *Lawrenceville Gazette*, just in case I'd misunderstood or he'd gotten it wrong. But the situation was exactly as Mr. Xian had said. "Nobody is running against this Lucinda person. Which means she will *definitely* be elected mayor, which means she will *definitely* stop paying for us to have art."

"Someone should run against her," Janet said.

"Janet, I cannot survive school without art! I *can't!*" I rolled down my window, because the very idea made me feel hot and claustrophobic.

SCHOOL IS HORRIBLE!

I don't have any friends there. (Except My Friend Daniel, but he'd dump me immediately if anyone better was willing to be friends with him.)

Teachers treat us like we're prisoners.
They yell at us for going to the bathroom
when we have to pea or eating food when
we're hungry.

I never do things the "right" way.
Kids think I'm being weird, and
teachers think I'm being rebellious.

"The *only* thing that makes school bearable is art," I told Janet. "That's *it*. And now the mayor is going to take that away from me?!"

I kicked my feet like a little kid throwing a tantrum and accidentally stubbed my toe on the bottom of the glove box. Then I yelled, "Ow, ow, ow!" a few times, because it hurt, and because it felt good to be loud.

Janet stopped at a red light and didn't say anything. She just looked sad.

"Janet!" I shouted. "You're supposed to tell me not to yell and kick!"

She shrugged. "I don't care if you yell and kick. I'd do the same. But you know it won't fix anything. What are you going to do about this new mayor?"

"There's nothing I *can* do." I realized it was true as I said it, and I let my head fall back against my seat. "I'm just a kid."

"So what?" Janet asked.

"So *everything*. I get no say in any of this. I can't stop Lucinda Burghart from becoming mayor, because I can't even vote yet. When she makes school even worse than it already is, I can't just quit seventh grade. I can't hire Mr.

Xian or buy good art supplies on my own, because I have no money. I'm *trapped.*"

"That sounds very defeatist," Janet said, turning right onto my street.

"Oh, I'm *so* sorry," I said. "I'll try to be more positive about the fact that someone who I don't even know, who doesn't even know me, is about to destroy my life for *no reason!*"

"That's an idea," Janet said as she pulled into the driveway.

"What, being positive? Janet, I was being sarcastic."

"No, I mean trying to meet Lucinda Burghart. Maybe if she *knew* you, she'd understand why this new policy would hurt you, and if she liked you, then she wouldn't *want* to hurt you. Right? Maybe she doesn't have any kids or grandkids, so she doesn't get it. Maybe if she really *saw* and *understood* one of the people her plan would affect, it would change her mind."

"Are you sure?" I asked. "Because I'm pretty sure she's just, like, evil."

"I have no idea," Janet said as she turned off the car, "but there is only one way to find out."

CHAPTER 4

The next day was rainy, so Janet was pleased, both because she'd correctly predicted it and because rain is one of her top five favorite weathers. She drove My Friend Daniel and me from school to the Lawrenceville Women's Club and parked right across the street, but our umbrellas and our shoes still got soaked in the time it took us to run inside.

We were there for something called a town hall, which is apparently a forum for citizens to meet with government candidates or officials and ask them questions. There weren't that many citizens at this town hall, though. I guess most people figured that there was no point in asking the candidate questions when no one was running against her, so she was going to become mayor no matter how she answered.

"I thought we were going to hang out today," Daniel whispered to me as he looked around the room.

"We *are* hanging out," I pointed out.

"Yes, but I thought we were going to hang out at your house. Or the park. Or Jordan's."

"Daniel, *why* would you think we were going to hang out at Jordan's?" Jordan's Hot House is this magical wonderland where dreams come true; it's a pizzeria and ice cream shop that has arcade games and lasers and candy. "We're not cool enough to hang out at Jordan's," I reminded him.

"Speak for yourself," Daniel said. "Anyway, I didn't know we were going to some kind of *political* meeting."

"It's not so bad," I said unconvincingly.

One of the old men in the audience chose that moment to ask, "My name is Edwin Barker, and what I want to know is, what are you going to do about that big pothole in front of the bank on Main Street? That pothole has been there for four years, and it's only getting worse. My daughter blew out her tire in it last spring, and did the city take responsibility? No, ma'am."

My Friend Daniel rolled his eyes at me, and I rolled mine right back. "It's pretty bad," he mouthed.

Lucinda Burghart stood at the podium at the front of the room, and she began to answer the question.

"Let me tell you a story," Lucinda Burghart said to Edwin. "When I was in the Olympics in '88, we showed up, all the way from this great country of America, and the locker room for our training pool hadn't been completed. No curtains on the shower stalls, missing tiles on the floor.

"Now, we could have complained. We could have kicked up a real fuss. Some of the girls wanted to. But I said, 'We're not here to talk. We're here to make history.' And I stand by that today, Edwin. I'm not here to *talk* about fixing that pothole. I am here to fix it."

She paused as though waiting for applause.

"What?" My Friend Daniel whispered to me.

Nobody else said *What?* so I wondered if Lucinda's answer actually made sense to them. Maybe this was just another one of those instances of everyone understanding something I didn't, but personally I had no idea what locker rooms from thirty years ago had to do with our broken roads. I suspected Lucinda had just brought it up so she had an excuse to mention that she was once in the Olympics.

Which was impressive, I had to admit. I didn't know anyone else who'd ever been in the Olympics. My aunt was once in the audience at the Olympic speed skating trials, but that wasn't really the same.

"Do we have any other questions?" Lucinda asked. "I *want* to hear your concerns. I want to make Lawrenceville into the great city that we all know it can and should be."

I really did not want to say anything. For starters, if Lucinda answered my questions like she'd an answered Edwin Barker's, it wouldn't help. Furthermore, it was kind of nerve-racking and embarrassing to stand up in front of a room full of adult strangers and tell them my concerns. What if they made fun of me or thought I was stupid just because I was a kid? What if I *did* accidentally say something stupid with everyone watching?

But I reminded myself that my question couldn't possibly be any stupider than that guy's question about a pothole. And also, I had come here to make my case for art. It didn't matter if I felt awkward or anxious. I *needed* to do this, because if I didn't, then my school, my life, my *everything* would be empty.

I stood up.

"Oh, hello, sweetheart," Lucinda Burghart said in a singsongy voice, like I was about half as old as I actually was. "What's *your* name?"

"I'm Maddie Polansky." I knotted my hands in front of me. "Um, I wanted to ask you . . ."

"Can you speak up, Maddie, honey?" Lucinda said, still in that high baby voice.

"Sorry." I cleared my throat. "I wanted to ask about, um, defunding arts education." I paused for a moment, but then I thought about how that pothole guy just kept going without any encouragement, so I kept talking, too. "I heard that you're planning to fire the art teachers and stop offering art and music and theater classes in schools. I'm very concerned about it. I know you're the one who came up with it, so you probably don't want to hear this, but I think it's a really, *really* bad idea.

"I wasn't sure if you'd talked to any kids about your plan to cut arts funding. Maybe you just asked the principals or parents or something. So I thought a kid should tell you that it's not a good idea for us."

Lucinda Burghart gave a little laugh—"Tee-hee," it sounded like—and silently applauded. "Thank you, Maddie," she said. "How inspiring to see Lawrenceville's youth getting involved in governance. Your intelligence and confidence are testaments to the strength and value of our public school system. And once I am mayor, that school system will be even stronger.

"My number-one priority is to cut taxes for ordinary working people, like most of us in this room. Now, Maddie, you're too young to pay taxes, so you can't really understand what it's like. Imagine it this way. Do you get an allowance?"

"Yes," I said. "Five dollars a week."

"Now imagine that every week, you had to give a dollar fifty of your five dollars to the government," Lucinda said. "So now you only get to keep three fifty. How does that make you feel?"

I frowned. "Bad," I said. "But what happens to the dollar fifty that I gave up?"

"The government has it," Lucinda explained in an *I already told you* voice.

"I know," I said, "but why? What is the government doing with it?"

"They're funding public services. And some of those services are necessary, of course. We need firefighters and police officers. We need stoplights that work and streets that are paved. It will be my job as mayor to cut the services we *don't* need that are costing the government money. Do we need libraries to purchase dozens of brand-new copies of every book? No! Do we need to run buses that nobody is riding? No! Do we need to pay for children to spend their school days on time-consuming amuse-ments that will never get them careers? We do not! That money is going back to *you*, the people of Lawrenceville!"

She kept saying *no* like it was obvious, like you must be stupid if you couldn't see this truth that was so clear to her. And maybe I was stupid. But I *couldn't* see it. Art wasn't a "time-consuming amusement" for me. It was my life.

And what did she mean, that art was never going to get me a career? Cartoonists had to start somewhere, didn't they? Mr. Xian had studied art as a kid, and being our teacher was a career, wasn't it?

"But—" I said.

"I know it's a child's job to complain about school," Lucinda said. "This might be hard to believe, but I was once your age myself! So I do think what you're doing is very cute. But we can't do what's wrong for our city just because *you* don't like it, little girl."

Cute? *Cute?!*

"I need art class," I whispered. My throat felt tight, so it was hard to make the words come out.

"Children don't know what's best for them," Lucinda announced to the room. "That's why they need a more focused school day. So they can learn what they need! Next question?"

Someone else stood up then and started talking about affordable housing, so I slowly sat down, my eyes fixed on my hands. I felt Janet's hand on my back, but I couldn't look at her.

This wasn't right. How could a person who didn't know anything about me claim to know what was best for me? How dare she tell me that my passion was "cute"? Lucinda hadn't listened to me at all. She already had her mind made up, and she wasn't going to change it no matter what I said or how good my argument was.

If I couldn't talk her out of her devious plan, then I had only one option:

CHAPTER 5

The only way to stop Lucinda from winning the race and enacting her evil plan was to find someone to beat her. Unfortunately, nobody could beat her when nobody was even running against her.

It was time to take matters into my own hands.

"I'm going to run for mayor of Lawrenceville," I announced to Mr. Xian. I paused, then asked, "Do you think anyone will vote for me?"

At school, most elections weren't really about who would do the best job. They just turned into popularity contests. So I'd never entered a school election before, because I didn't need a formal contest to find out that I wasn't popular. I hoped mayoral elections didn't work the same way.

Mr. Xian smiled at me. "I bet lots of people would vote for you if they could," he said, "but they can't."

"Why not?"

"Because the law says you have to be over eighteen to run for elected office in this state."

But I wasn't giving up that easily. Fortunately, I lived with two people over the age of eighteen.

I started with Mom. She was in the basement, getting ready for a workout webinar.

"Can I talk to you?" I asked.

"I'm pretty busy right now, honey," she told me as she stretched out her arms. "Can you talk to Janet instead?"

"Janet's not here. She's at a job fair. You gave her the evening off. Remember?"

"That girl really should get a job," Mom agreed, rotating her neck around like an owl. "Twenty-three and still living with her parents? That's no good, no good at all. I read a fascinating article about this exact topic the other day. This whole generation, they're going to college, getting these useless degrees, and then moving right back home. They have some name for it. 'The Lost Generation,' I think. Maybe it was a different name. It sounded very depressing, whatever it was."

"I know," I said. "Janet knows, too. That's why she's at this job fair. She wants to get a job that has to do with weather, maybe. Or maybe not, because she says it's not always a good idea to monetize your passions."

"Sure," Mom said. She laid out her yoga mat. "Just as long as she doesn't get too busy to take care of you. I was so impressed when you told me she took you to that political event yesterday."

"The town hall," I supplied.

"What a fascinating enrichment opportunity for Janet to come up with for you. I've always intended to go to one of those. Really get *involved* in the community, you know? But I just have so much going on. There aren't enough hours in a day, Maddie."

"I guess. It depends on the day," I replied. "Some days are way too long."

Today had been one of those. In drama class we'd had to do some exercise where you mirrored the movements of your partner. Of course partner activities create a huge conflict for Holly and Molly and Polly, and they always beg to work as a threesome. And Mrs. Cheng usually lets Polly get away with whatever she wants, because Polly is the darling of the theater department and the lead in every play, so Mrs. Cheng bends over backward to make her happy.

But today Mrs. Cheng held firm, so Polly and Molly partnered up, and then My Friend Daniel saw his opportunity and swooped in to claim Holly as *his* partner. Good for him, but unfortunately My Friend Daniel and I were *already* partners for the exercise, so all of a sudden I didn't have a partner at all, and I wound up having to mirror Mrs. Cheng's movements.

"Mom?" I said now, as she arranged her pairs of weights in front of her. "Are you going to vote for Lucinda Burghart for mayor?"

"I imagine I will," she replied. "She's been on the city council for years, and it seems like she's always done a fine job. I don't even know who's running against her, to be honest."

"No one is running against her," I said.

"Well, there you have it."

"What if she wanted to do something bad, though?" I asked.

"Like what?"

"She said that if she's elected, she'll cut funding for a ton of good things. Like art classes."

"Hmm." Mom rotated her arms forward, then backward. "Politicians make a lot of campaign promises, Maddie. They promise to do whatever they think people want, but often once they're elected, they don't go through with those things. Sometimes it turns out to be harder than they'd imagined to make changes. I wouldn't worry about it too much."

That gave me some hope. But I didn't feel all that relieved. "So what am I supposed to do, then? Just wait for her to get elected and keep my fingers crossed that she doesn't get around to doing what she promised?"

Mom kicked her leg up behind her and grabbed on to her ankle to stretch her quadriceps, and she sounded tired as she said, "I suppose so."

"Why do they even call it a campaign *promise*, anyway?" I went on. "Like, if I *promise* I'm going to watch the new season of *Killer Science* with My Friend Daniel,

I have to actually do it. Later I can't just be like, 'Oh, sorry, it turned out to be harder than I thought not to watch *Killer Science* the instant it comes out, so I guess my promise is meaningless now.'"

"A lot of politicians are unscrupulous," Mom agreed. "It's certainly not a job I would ever want."

"Are you sure?" I asked.

"Sure that politicians are unscrupulous?"

"Sure that you'd never want to be one," I said. "Like, don't you think it would be *fascinating* to be mayor? Don't you think it would be a real *enrichment opportunity?*"

Mom laughed like I was joking. "Maybe if I had more spare time."

"Are you ready?" shouted some voice from her phone. "Are you ready to get into the best shape. Of. Your. Liiiiiiife?"

"Ready!" Mom shouted, jumping into a squat position.

"When are you going to have more spare time?" I asked.

"Take a deep breath!" the workout guy shouted. "Breathe your arms all the way up! Over your head! That's it!"

"*Mom.*"

"I'll have time when I win the lottery or when I'm dead, whichever comes first. Now, Maddie, I need to—"

"SPRINT!" shouted the workout guy.

Mom was not going to be much help in my fight against Lucinda Burghart.

CHAPTER
6

I moved on to my next potential mayoral candidate: Dad. He was out in the garden, as usual.

"You think you can take over my garden," I heard Dad muttering at a plant as I approached. "'Oh, I'm a tree of heaven,' you think to yourself. 'I'm a big shot. I can grow wherever I want!' Well, tree of heaven, looks like you have finally met your match!"

I stood nearby for a couple of minutes and waited for Dad to notice me, but he was too engrossed in his battle of wits with the weed. "Dad," I said at last.

"Oh, hey, Maddie! You were so quiet I didn't even see you there, sweetheart. You've come out here just in time to see your old man triumph over this ingrown ingrate."

He snapped his shears at the plant with all the focus of an executioner. "Did you know that these leaves are poisonous?" he said, glaring at it.

Here is the important thing to know about my dad: He is wrong basically all of the time. Sometimes I think he's purposefully lying in order to make life sound more exciting. Most of the time, though, I think he genuinely doesn't remember details and just assumes everything is a bigger deal than it actually is.

So for this plant, for example, when he said that the leaves were poisonous, what I understood that to mean was that some leaves of some plants are definitely poisonous. Just possibly not *this* one.

"Hey, Daddy," I said, "I have a question. Would you run for mayor of Lawrenceville?"

Dad seemed to take this question much more seriously than Mom had. He looked thoughtful. "My old childhood friend became mayor of a major city. Miami, I think it was. He made some big changes there. Had a huge impact. Good man. Ever since we were kids, I knew he was cut out for that sort of work."

Translation: My dad once knew a guy who got elected to do something somewhere. They may not have been friends. The job may not have been mayor. It definitely wasn't in Miami.

"What about *you*, though?" I pressed. "Would *you* want to be mayor?"

"Oh, I don't think so," he said. "I usually don't even vote, to be honest."

"Why not?" I asked. If I could vote, I *definitely* would. Why would I purposely sit on my hands and let other people make decisions about my life? I got enough of that just by being twelve.

"I'm not that interested in politics," Dad said, bending down to pull up a weed. "And all politicians are pretty much the same. It doesn't really make a difference which one you vote for, or if you vote at all. It works out fine in the long run."

This seemed like one of the wrongest things my dad had said in a lifetime of saying wrong things. As usual, I didn't know for *sure* that he was wrong. But just based on what I'd seen at yesterday's town hall and what I'd read in the *Lawrenceville Gazette*, what he said didn't make much sense. Lucinda literally wanted different things from the current mayor. She was planning to change our city. Maybe that would work out fine for some people, like my dad. He didn't have to go to school, after all. But it wouldn't work out fine for everybody. And I knew that, because it wouldn't work out fine for *me*.

"So what do you do," I said, "if an elected official is trying to pass a law that you don't like? If you don't vote, then how do you stop them?"

"You can protest!" Dad replied with a flash of excite ment. "March, give speeches, write them letters. Civil disobedience—that's how you show them that they don't have any power over you. Have I ever told you about the time I handcuffed myself to a tree near my college that developers were going to cut down?"

"Wow," I said. "Did that work?"

"No." Dad sighed. "They cut it down anyway. But I'm sure my protest made them feel guilty about it."

"Oh."

"It was a good tree," Dad recalled, looking a little teary-eyed.

"Do you still march or give speeches or whatever?" I asked.

He stopped looked teary and shook his head. "Like I said, I don't really follow politics."

He even sounded a little bit proud of it.

It was time to face the facts: Not only did neither of my parents *want* to run for mayor, they'd also both be terrible at it. What I really needed was an adult who wasn't crazy, who had a lot of time, and who actually cared.

Now, where was I going to find one of those?

CHAPTER 7

"Do you want to run for mayor?" I asked Janet.

"Sure."

"I'm not joking," I told her.

"I know you're not."

It was the next day, and Janet was fixing an after-school snack for me and My Friend Daniel. I'd been thinking all day about how I could ask her to run against Lucinda, and I'd come up with all sorts of arguments and counterarguments. It never occurred to me that she'd just say *yes*.

"Because you need a job," I explained, even though it sounded like Janet didn't need much convincing. "And being mayor *is* a job. And you're registered to vote here, and you're over eighteen, so you meet all the requirements."

"I'd be happy to run for mayor," Janet said, setting a plate of apple slices and peanut butter down on the table. "It's not like I'm doing anything else with my life. But you know I won't *win*, right?"

"Why not?" I asked.

"Because I have absolutely zero experience in politics. I have no work experience at all, really, unless you count taking care of you, volunteering, and moderating the Weather or Not Weather News Board—which is, by the way, a *huge* job. But yeah. Nobody in Lawrenceville knows who I am."

"*Some* people know who you are," I pointed out. "We do."

"Lucinda has been on the city council for years," Janet said. "Everybody in town recognizes her name, and they trust her. She can point to her record of accomplishments, while I can point to, like . . . getting a sociology degree and living in my parents' house."

I knew that everything Janet was saying was true. But I *also* knew she would be a better mayor than Lucinda.

"Plus, Lucinda is an Olympian," My Friend Daniel

piped up, spreading peanut butter evenly over an apple slice, carefully making sure that no part of the apple was left bare.

"What does *that* have to do with anything?" I asked.

"Nothing. It's just cool, that's all. I wonder if we could see her medals."

WHAT LUCINDA'S MEDALS PROBABLY LOOK LIKE

"Lucinda doesn't have any medals," Janet said. She took a bite of apple. "I looked it up after she was bragging about it at the town hall. She came in second-to-last place in her event in 1988. Second-to-last at the Olympics is still better than not going to the Olympics at all, but . . ."

"What was her event?" My Friend Daniel asked. "Was she a snowboarder?"

"She did something called solo synchronized swimming," Janet replied grimly.

"I thought synchronized swimming meant that you had to swim *in sync* with somebody else," I said.

"It does," Janet confirmed.

"So what is *solo* synchronized swimming?"

"Does that just mean you have to swim in sync with, like, *yourself*?" Daniel asked.

"Apparently, yes."

Even I think this is a weird sport.

"That doesn't make any sense," said Daniel, looking deeply disappointed that the first Olympian he'd ever met had turned out to be such a dud.

"It was only an Olympic sport for a few years before they noticed that it didn't make sense and got rid of it," said Janet. "According to the internet."

"You see?" I exclaimed. "Janet, you would definitely make a better mayor than a solo synchronized swimmer, which is *not a thing!*"

"I agree," said Daniel. "I'd *really* wanted Lucinda to be a snowboarder."

I leaned over Janet's shoulder as she pulled out her phone and typed in "how to run for mayor of Lawrenceville." The board of elections website came up, and it had a bunch of information and deadlines.

"We have to go to City Hall," Janet read, "and fill out a form to declare my candidacy."

"Can we go now?" I asked.

Janet checked the time. "It says they're open until five, and it's only four now. So we can go today if we hurry. Why not?"

See, this is what I like about Janet. My parents never do anything "now." My mom would be like, "Sounds like a

great idea—let me put it on my calendar for next month."
And then she'd wind up cancelling anyway.

We got to City Hall and went inside. There was a
chandelier overhead in the rotunda and a few stained
glass windows. We approached the security desk, and I
asked the guy there, "Where do you register to run for
political office?"

I thought he might laugh at me or say, "Why do *you*
need to know how to run for political office?" But he just

smiled pleasantly and said, "City clerk's office—just down that hallway, five doors down on the left."

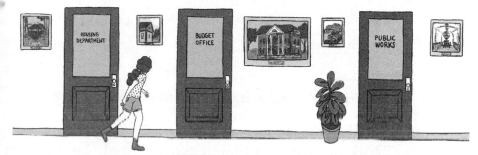

When we got to the city clerk's office, we were greeted by a man around my dad's age seated at a computer at the reception desk. Behind him I could see a few other people working away at their computers, a couple of people on the phone, one making photocopies, and another sifting through a box of Dunkin' Donuts munchkins that had been left on a table.

"How can I help you?" the reception guy asked.

"We want to sign up to run for mayor," Daniel announced.

"Not *all* of us," I clarified. "Just her." I pointed at Janet.

"Hi," said Janet.

"Now?" the guy asked. He sounded surprised.

"Yes," I said.

"Unless you think there's some reason why we should

wait . . . ?" Janet said, looking surprised by his surprise.

"No, no," he said. "The opposite of that, actually. It's just—you know that the window to file petitions to run for mayor has been open for six weeks, right? It closes on Monday."

"Well, then it's a good thing we didn't wait until Monday!" Daniel said.

"That's true," the receptionist acknowledged, "but it only gives you three days to gather your signatures."

"Signatures?"

"Why?" Daniel asked.

"Because it shows that you're capable of running a real campaign," the receptionist said. "If all you had to do was write down your name, hundreds or thousands of people might 'run' for mayor, and most of them wouldn't actually do any work. You have to clear this bar—and it's a pretty low bar—to show that you're taking it seriously."

"It's not *that* low of a bar," Daniel said. "Where are we supposed to find three hundred and fifty people?"

"There are way more than that many kids at school," I pointed out.

"All of them have to be registered voters in Lawrenceville, though," the man reminded us. "That means eighteen or over."

That was so unfair!

"And it has to be their in-person signatures?" Janet asked. "I can't just ask everyone I went to high school with to email me?"

"In-person," he confirmed. "This is why we give candidates six weeks to collect their signatures." He pointed at the calendar and shrugged, like there was nothing to be done about it.

Janet and I looked at each other in dismay.

"Can it be done in three days?" Janet asked the man.

"I have no idea," he said, handing the forms to her. "But you can certainly try."

CHAPTER 8

Three hundred and fifty signatures. Three days. We could do this, Janet and Daniel and I, if we divided and conquered.

Personally I did not actually *have* a signature because I never actually 100 percent learned cursive. Unless you're signing your name on a political petition, when are you ever going to use it? Most people's signatures just look like scribbles and I suspect that's because *nobody* ever really learned cursive.

On Friday, I asked every grown-up I saw. I started with my parents as they were drinking their morning tea. "Can you sign this?" I put the form down on the table in front of them.

Mom laughed. "Maddie, you crack me up. You honestly do." She signed her name. "How many signatures are you trying to get?"

"Three hundred and fifty."

"I can take a sheet to my office," she offered, "and get some of my colleagues to sign. Bill?"

"Sure," Dad said, taking a page from me. "I'll ask around."

"Is this for a school project?" Mom asked me.

"What do you mean?"

"For social studies or something? Your class is learning about how the democratic process works? I remember doing something like that when I was in middle school. We had a mock election and did everything just like it was real. We campaigned and debated and voted, the whole bit. It was terrific fun."

I can never be sure if my mom actually loved middle school as much as she says she did—which would be horrible, because that would mean she must have been one of the normal kids when she was my age—or whether she just can't remember how bad it was and assumes she must have liked it. Or maybe she knows that it was miserable and is just lying to me about how awesome it can be because she hopes I'll believe her and not my own life experiences.

"Yes," I said. "It is a very fun school project. But also, wouldn't it be great if Janet *did* get elected?"

Mom laughed again and kissed the top of my head. "It would be wonderful," she said.

When I got to school, instead of sitting in the corner and doodling while I waited for first period to begin, I started collecting signatures from every adult I could find.

Sign my petition!

The crossing guard!

The attendance secretary!

The bus coordinator!

The maintenance man!

I don't even know who this lady is!

"How many do you have?" I asked My Friend Daniel when we met up before first period.

"Ten." He showed me his list.

"I have twelve. But look, we got four of the same people from the front office. So we actually only have . . . eighteen."

We stared at each other in dismay.

"We've just started," I reminded him. "We never thought this was going to be easy."

"I kind of thought it would be easy," Daniel volunteered.

"Okay, well, you were deluding yourself. Let's go."

In the afternoon, I got lucky: There was an all-school assembly. Usually I hate assembly because kids fight over the good seats, and they fight to sit next to their friends, and I don't like fighting, so I always end up in some uncomfortable folding chair where I can't see anything, next to boys who are purposely burping as loudly as possible while the assembly speaker lectures us on the power of positive thinking or whatever.

But today, assembly was exactly what I needed, since it was forty-five minutes when basically everyone in the entire school was together.

I ran around to every teacher I could get to before we had to sit down. On the opposite side of the room, I saw My Friend Daniel doing the same thing. I collected signatures from teachers for the other grades and teachers for classes I didn't even take, like French and orchestra.

Not everybody signed. Some of the teachers were so occupied with trying to keep their classes in order that they could barely give me any attention, let alone write down their information. A few said that even though they worked in Lawrenceville, they didn't *live* there, so their signatures wouldn't count. Mr. Xian fell into that category. But he loved that I was trying to get Janet on the ballot. "Go get 'em!" he told me.

I fidgeted all through assembly, eager to get back to

collecting signatures. Since this was the first assembly of the school year, we didn't have an outside speaker. Instead, the theme was "Get Involved!" which meant that every extracurricular group had ninety seconds to introduce themselves and try to convince people to join.

BAND!

I think they're supposed to be playing a Beatles medley? Honestly, it's hard to tell.

Of course the drama club just put Polly up onstage and let her belt out her solo from the school musical last spring. It was annoying.

I mean, Polly is actually a very good performer, and I saw her in the musical twice last year and almost cried both times.

But it was still annoying.

When the school day ended, I quickly rounded up a few last signatures from some of the after-school sports coaches, and then I ran out to the front, where Janet was already parked and waiting for me outside her car. "How many did you get?" she asked me.

"Seventy-three," I said, coming to a panting halt beside her.

"Maddie, that's a ton! Nice work! I got fifty-six."

"And I got thirty," My Friend Daniel said, running up to us. "I would have gotten more, but Maddie asked a lot of my people first."

"So all together we're at"—I did the math—"one hundred and fifty-nine."

We looked at one another.

"So we're not even halfway there?" Daniel made a face. "I don't think there's a single adult at school we haven't asked already!"

"We're only a few hours into it," Janet reassured him. "We still have all weekend."

"I know," he said, "but tomorrow I have to go up to my grandmother's, so I might not talk to anybody who lives in Lawrenceville at all."

"Can you go door-to-door tonight and ask your neighbors?" I suggested.

Daniel gave a long sigh, like he was doing us a huge favor. "I guess so. But I don't know two hundred neighbors."

"Let's all go to the farmers market on Sunday," Janet said. "I'm predicting a sunny day in the high seventies, not too much wind. Perfect weather for people to be outdoors, so the market should be packed. We can ask everybody there to sign."

I widened my eyes at her. "You don't take care of me on weekends, though."

"I know, but don't you think your parents will let you come with me anyway?"

"Yeah," I said. "But they won't pay you for it, because they don't need you this weekend."

"What do I care?" asked Janet. "*I* need *you* this weekend."

"Oh," I said, feeling surprised and pleased. "Okay, then."

CHAPTER 9

Sunday was a beautiful late-summer day, as Janet had predicted, but there was a sense of unease in the air, because if we didn't finish getting our 350 signatures that day, we would be out of the race before it even started.

Maybe I was the only one sensing unease in the air, though. Everybody else at the farmers market seemed to be having a low-stress day of tasting Mutsu apples and watching composting demonstrations.

People at the farmers market were less willing to stop and talk to me than the teachers at school had been. I guess because they didn't know who I was, and maybe they weren't used to interacting with kids.

I got a couple around Janet's age to sign the petition,

but after they walked off, I saw that they'd both put down their names as "Poopy McPoopster" and their addresses as "1 Poop Lane." I didn't need to look at a map to figure out that I couldn't count them toward our 350.

Most people weren't mean about saying no. A lot of them said they were sorry. But they were all in a rush

to be somewhere, or at least they acted like they were in a rush as soon as they saw me coming toward them with my clipboard. And it was hard to keep going up to people when they just kept on rejecting me. Every time I approached a stranger I had to psych myself up a little, and the more people said no or just ignored me, the less psyching-up energy I had left inside me.

"You've got to lead with what you're petitioning *for*," said a guy with a thick beard and a head full of dreadlocks, coming up beside me. He was carrying a clipboard of his own. "You only get someone's attention for one second before they move on to the next thing. So think hard about what you're going to say in that first second to convince them to give you *another* second, and then another. Like this." He turned to an older guy who was walking past, carrying a basil plant in his arms, and said, "Hey, man, how do you feel about climate change?"

The basil plant guy smiled at him and kept walking.

"Like that?" I said dryly.

"Sometimes it works, sometimes it doesn't," the clipboard guy said with a shrug. He didn't seem that bothered. "I've been out here protesting fossil fuels every weekend since before you were born, kid. Some weeks are better than others, but I always get enough signatures to make it worth my while."

You've been trying to stop climate change every weekend for more than twelve years?

A lot more than twelve years.

And it still hasn't happened?

"We've made some progress," he said. "But until this entire country lowers its carbon footprint, I'll be out here."

"But don't you ever feel, like . . ." I paused, because I didn't want to say anything that would make him feel bad. "Discouraged?" I finished at last. "Like you've put in all this effort, and it hasn't really gotten any better?"

"Nah," he said. "Because if I *hadn't* put in that effort, then it would have gotten so much *worse.*"

I supposed that could be true.

"Furthermore," he said, "if you want something, you've got to go after it. It doesn't matter if you think you're never going to get there, because you for sure won't get there if you don't even try. Proceed boldly toward your dreams! Even if you never arrive at the destination, at least you'll be headed in the right direction."

"Okay," I said. "So will you sign my petition?"

"Sure." He uncapped his pen. "What's it for?"

"It's to get Janet Teneman on the ballot for mayor."

"Who's Janet Teneman?" he asked.

"She's my friend." Then, in case it sounded like I was making that up, I added, "And my babysitter."

"Right on," he said. He signed his name—Ayodele Okereke—then put his pen back in his shirt pocket. "Good luck to you and Janet, kid."

"Good luck to you, too."

After Mr. Okereke walked off, I approached two women who were considering the cheese options while a boy who looked a few years younger than me hung out behind them, watching a video on a phone. I thought about Mr. Okereke's advice, and I started with, "Do you think it's a bad idea to get rid of arts education in schools?"

The women kind of smiled at me and otherwise ignored me. "I don't think we need Swiss *and* Gouda," one of them said to the other. "We should complement a hard cheese with a soft one."

But the boy lowered his phone to gape at me. "Do you mean like video game design?" he asked. "Do you mean we *wouldn't get to do video game design?*"

"That's what the person who's going to be mayor next year will do." I held up my clipboard "*If* we don't get enough signatures to stop her."

He immediately started tugging at the women's shirts. "Mom," he said. "Mama. Sign this thing. Sign it right now."

And, just like that, they did.

And that gave me a brilliant idea.

So that was what I did for the next two hours of the farmers market. I talked to every kid I saw. "Can you get your parents to sign this petition?" I asked. "Tell them it doesn't cost any money. Tell them they don't have to do anything except sign their name and address. It's the only way to stop the city from getting rid of art at school."

I sized up the kids as they approached, trying to notice specific details to help me craft my argument. When

I saw a girl in a leotard, her hair in a bun, I said, "The next mayor wants to get rid of dancing!" and when I saw a boy engrossed in a book, I told him, "The mayor is going to eliminate creative writing programs in our schools!"

Not everyone stopped and got their parents to sign. But a lot of them did.

It was by far the most kids I'd ever spoken to on purpose. Sometimes there were full days where the only person my age I chose to speak to was My Friend Daniel. But today I was talking to *everyone*.

"You're a real go-getter," the cheese lady said to me at 3:00 p.m., as she began to disassemble her booth. She gave me another piece of cheese, but this one was really smelly. I didn't want to be rude, so I just said, "Thanks," took a tiny bite, and then subtly stuck the rest in my pocket.

I met up with Janet and Daniel at the main entrance to the market. "Did we do it?" Daniel asked, hopping from foot to foot. "Did we get enough?"

We sat down on the grass and started counting signatures. It took a while, because we had to figure out which ones were fakes (like the Poopy McPoopsters) and which were duplicates. We kept getting confused and asking questions like, "Is this Michael Smith's handwriting the same as that Michael Smith's handwriting?" and having to start over.

But finally we figured it all out. We went back to the first page of the petition and did one last final count of every single signature.

CHAPTER 10

THE LAWRENCEVILLE GAZETTE

NEW CANDIDATE ADDS NAME TO MAYORAL BALLOT

On Monday, the candidate list for mayor of Lawrenceville was finalized. With current mayor Enrique Peñate retiring at the end of this term, the seat is wide open.

As of last weekend, it looked like City Alderwoman Lucinda Burghart would be the only one on the ballot. But Monday—the final day to submit nomination paperwork—brought a surprise, with political newcomer Janet Teneman stepping into the ring.

Little is known about Teneman, who is twenty-three and grew up in Lawrenceville, graduating from Lawrenceville High School before receiving her degree in sociology from Drexel University. She is a volunteer for the City Parks Department, a nanny for a local family, and the moderator for what appears to be an online community that talks exclusively about the weather.

In a phone interview, Teneman told the *Gazette*, "I'm proud be a Lawrencevillian. There are so many things I think this city is doing right. At the same time, I have lots of ideas for things we can do even better. I want to focus on our education system. It wasn't that long ago that I went to school here, which gives me a unique perspective. And I want to protect and expand our public park land."

When told of her new opponent, Burghart was quoted as saying, "How wonderful to see such a very, *very* young person showing interest in the political process. Of course, when I was her age, I was just coming back from competing in the Olympics, so I can't even imagine what it would be like to be so young and have the free time to run for mayor. As far as I'm aware, Janet Teneman is not an Olympian and has never held political office, so I suppose we have led very different lives. This race will give the voting public a clear choice, that's for sure!"

The two candidates will meet in a debate hosted by the League of Women Voters on October 10. Election Day is Tuesday, November 8.

It was really cool, seeing Janet's name in the *Lawrenceville Gazette* like that. And even cooler because I was sort of in there, too, in the line where it said that Janet was "a nanny for a local family." They meant me. I'd never called Janet a nanny before, just a babysitter, and I didn't know what the difference was except that "nanny" sounded more official. Which was maybe why the newspaper had used that word instead, so it sounded more like Janet had an actual job and not like she just came over to my house sometimes.

Not everybody seemed to find this article interesting, though. We each had to bring in news articles for social studies, and that was mine, but nobody wanted to talk about it. Mostly they had questions for Polly, who'd brought in a newspaper review of a Beyoncé concert that she'd gone to.

After social studies ended, My Friend Daniel and I walked to our next class together. "I've been thinking," he said, which is never a good start to a sentence from Daniel, because in the past he's been thinking things like "I should give my dog a haircut," and "You should hide and I can tell your parents you were kidnapped."

"I've been thinking," Daniel went on, "that I should be less involved in Janet's campaign."

"What do you mean, *less* involved? The campaign literally just began. Were you even listening to my news article?"

"Yeah," he said, "but it feels like I've already done a lot of work, and I just don't know that it's my priority right now."

"Oh, really? What exactly *is* your priority right now, then?"

"Well," My Friend Daniel said in this trying-not-to-brag tone, "I made the soccer team."

"Oh!" I said. "Congratulations." I'd never actually seen Daniel play soccer outside of gym class, but maybe he was secretly some kind of soccer genius. Maybe he had this natural gift for it that he had denied all his life, but it was in there all along, just yearning to break free.

"Thanks," Daniel said in that same tone of voice. "I mean, it's the Yellow Team, so I don't want to make *too* big a deal about it—"

"Hold up," I said, stopping so suddenly that a sixth grader almost crashed into me. "*Yellow?* Daniel, that's not even a team."

For most sports, our school just has a Red Team, which is the good team, and an Orange Team, which is the less-good team. For really popular sports like soccer, they sometimes add a Yellow Team, which is for everyone who not only isn't talented enough to make Red but who can't even make Orange.

"All the teams are equal," Daniel said stubbornly. "I just got randomly assigned to Yellow. Maybe they knew it's my favorite color."

"All the teams are *not* equal. Red gets full uniforms, and they play at States. Yellow gets bandanas and doesn't get to play anyone except one another."

I didn't say anything. Because here's the thing: I *do* want more friends. I just don't know how to find them.

I don't have anything in common with the other kids at school. They're all like boring clones of one another.

They care so much about stuff that just seems dumb to me. And I guess the stuff I care about seems dumb to them, too.

Maybe there are people like me somewhere out there in the world, and maybe someday I'll meet them. But they're not at Lawrenceville Middle School.

"No one cares about this election," My Sort-Of Friend Daniel told me. "Like, you just brought in that article about it, and nobody cared *at all*."

"Yeah, okay, I noticed that, thank you."

"So *I* don't want to get too involved in it," he concluded.

"So you care about soccer because other people care about soccer," I said, just to make sure, "but you don't care about defeating Lucinda Burghart because other people don't care about that."

"Yeah . . ." My Friend Daniel rolled his eyes up toward the ceiling thoughtfully. "It sounds kind of bad when you say it that way. I dunno why."

"But don't you care that if we lose, we won't get to do anything creative at school?" I demanded. "It'll all be textbooks and standardized test prep and memorization and reports. Doesn't that bother you?"

"Of course it does."

"Just not enough to do anything about it," I concluded. "Not enough to put in effort or to make anyone think you care too much about something that they don't care about."

My Friend Daniel shrugged, and now it was his turn to look down at the floor.

"Great," I said. "Well, when school is even more strict and boring and gray than it already is, I hope you feel like you made the right choice."

And I turned around and marched into math class.

CHAPTER 11

I was in a rotten mood later that day as I sat in the kitchen eating the after-school snack Janet had fixed for me and scribbling angry, thick pen marks all over my sketch pad. I was annoyed with Daniel for caring more about his barely-a-soccer-team than he did about our future. And I was even more annoyed with him for being right: Nobody *did* seem interested in this election except for Janet and me. And as she and I started looking into what it actually took to run a successful political campaign, it was suddenly seeming like . . . a lot.

Janet had stepped outside to take a phone call, leaving me sitting alone with the information we'd found about the stages of a political campaign.

How exactly were we supposed to achieve all of that? Tens of thousands of voters lived in Lawrenceville. We'd never be able to reach them all. Especially considering there were only three of us working on Janet's campaign. Really two and a half, since My Friend Daniel only kind of counted.

I threw my pen down and started to head outside to see if Janet was off her phone call so she could tell me what we should do. But I paused at the door when I heard her tone of voice. She sounded upset.

"I don't know what to tell you," I heard her say to whomever was on the other end. "It was a long time ago, and I was a lot younger then. I don't think it has anything to do with who I am today." She paused, listening. "Yes, I would," she said, then paused to listen again. "Why? Because as mayor, I'd do what's right for Lawrenceville. And if someone doesn't want to vote for me because of a mistake I made when I was a kid, well . . . that's their choice, I suppose, but I think that's ridiculous." She cleared her throat. "Yes," she said. "Okay. Thanks for calling. Bye."

She put her phone in her pocket and opened the door

to come back inside. Then she saw me standing right there, looking at her.

"Hey, Maddie," she said.

"What mistake did you make when you were a kid?" I asked. "Who was that? Are you okay? You sounded upset."

She gave me a weak, unhappy smile. "That was a reporter from the *Gazette*. They heard . . . something about me, and they're about to run a story about it, and they wanted to get a quote from me first."

"What did they hear about you?" I asked. Whatever it was, clearly it was nothing good. But I couldn't imagine what it might be. I'd known Janet since I was a little kid, and I'd never heard anything not-good about her. How could the *Lawrenceville Gazette* know something that I didn't?

"Let's sit down." I followed Janet back into the kitchen and slid into the seat across from her. She rested her chin in her hands. "When I was fourteen," she began, "I cheated in English class."

"You did?" I jerked back to look at her.

She nodded. "Here's what happened . . ."

We were supposed to write an essay on <u>To Kill a Mockingbird</u> and I kept putting off reading it.

Eventually it was right before the essay was due, and I'd still read only a few chapters of the book. I hadn't told anyone that I was having trouble, and now I was too far behind to get caught up.

My teacher was really strict. He was always threatening to fail us for being late. I'd never failed <u>anything</u>, and I didn't know what to do.

I stayed up the whole night before the paper was due. I looked online for information about the book that I could use for my essay. Then I came across someone else's essay. And I just... copied it and put my name on it and handed it in.

"You plagiarized?" I whispered.

"Yes. Just that one time—not that it's okay to do even once. The teacher checked everyone's essays for plagiarism, so of course he caught me. He was angry, my parents were furious, and I felt so guilty. I failed the class."

"How come I didn't know about this?" I demanded.

"You were really little," she reminded me.

"Yes, but how come you never told me since then?"

Janet sighed. "It was almost ten years ago. It has nothing to do with who I am today. I shouldn't have done it, I made up for it, and I haven't done anything like it since. It was a horrible decision, and I learned my lesson."

"So how did the *Gazette* find out about it?"

"I imagine my old teacher told them when he heard that I was running for mayor. Or maybe someone else told the reporter—one of the other kids in my class, or one of the other teachers. A lot of people knew about it at the time, because I got in trouble and the school wanted to make an example of me. I don't know how many of them would still remember and care about it a decade later.

"But now the *Gazette* is going to run an article about it. They talked to Lucinda before they called me, and she said that an unqualified cheater shouldn't be mayor. She said that I didn't do the work for that class, and I won't do the work for our city. She said that she didn't cheat at the Olympics. The reporter wanted to know if I had anything to say about any of that." Janet closed her eyes, like it hurt to look at the world.

I felt like crying from frustration. "*Why* did you have to cheat?"

"I just told you," she said. "I had poor judgment. I shouldn't have—"

I felt like crying. Janet had betrayed me—she had betrayed me *years* ago, and I hadn't even known it.

"I'm not perfect," Janet said gently. "I never claimed to be. I cheated in school one time. I can't find a job. I don't have any money saved. I'm mean to my dad sometimes. I got a parking ticket a month ago and haven't paid it yet. I'm not a terrible person, but I'm certainly not perfect."

"But you're *supposed* to be," I repeated desperately.

"I wish I could be the person you want me to be, Maddie," Janet said. "I love seeing myself through your eyes. You think I'm smart and brave and sophisticated and good at everything, and I *want* to be all of that for you. I don't ever want to disappoint you."

"So don't disappoint me, then," I muttered.

"Too late." She rubbed her hands across her face. "Look, I didn't tell you that I once plagiarized an essay because I didn't want you to think any less of me, okay? I wanted you to keep seeing me the way you always have—as the person who can do anything, the superhero babysitter who can save the day, who can take on the bad guys, who could even become mayor. I wanted to be that person. But I'm just . . . not."

"Does this mean you can't be mayor?" I asked.

"Well, already probably nobody was going to vote for me except for my parents. Once this news gets out there . . . still nobody's going to vote for me except for my parents."

"Are you *giving up?*" She couldn't be. Not when there was so much left to do. Not when I needed her. When *all kids* needed her.

"Maybe?" Janet said in a small voice.

I sucked in my breath. "The thing is, I didn't really think about what it would mean to run for mayor. That all my private stuff, decisions I made years ago, would get dragged out into the spotlight for everyone to see and judge. It feels invasive and scary. I didn't know it was going to be like this.

"I'm sorry I let you down," Janet went on. "I'm sorry I let us *both* down. I would have liked to be mayor. But." And then she didn't say anything else. She didn't have to.

CHAPTER 12

THE LAWRENCEVILLE GAZETTE

NEW POLL SHOWS BURGHART WITH SIXTY-THREE-POINT LEAD

Election Day is still two months away, but victory already seems to be sewn up for Alderwoman Lucinda Burghart. Since her last-minute entry into the race, underdog Janet Teneman has made barely a peep. It's not clear if she's running an active campaign at all. In fact, the only news from Teneman's camp since she declared her candidacy concerns a cheating scandal from Teneman's high school years. "It was a long time ago, and I was a lot younger then," said Teneman, who failed a ninth-grade English class after plagiarizing an essay. "I don't think it has anything to do with who I am today."

Burghart feels differently. "Once a cheater, always a cheater," she told the *Gazette*. "Janet is a sweet little girl, but I wouldn't trust her with a school assignment, let alone with our very important city."

Part of the issue may be that Teneman, a recent college graduate, is not that much older now than she was when she was caught cheating.

A recent poll shows that 68 percent of voters say they are supporting Burghart, 5 percent say they are supporting Teneman, and the remaining 27 percent are undecided. When asked if she planned to ease up on the intensity of her campaign given her substantial lead, Burghart said no. "When I was in the Olympic Trials, I didn't go easy on my second routine even though I'd already nailed my first," she said. "I kept fighting for my personal best right up until the last moment."

I didn't hear from Janet at all over the weekend. As far as I could tell, she'd basically given up. We certainly weren't doing any of the things that the various internet articles said were necessary for running a successful campaign. And we were already behind where we were supposed to be two months before an election. It felt like I saw stuff about Lucinda everywhere I looked, but there was nothing out there about Janet.

On Monday, we had drama class, which would normally be one of the more fun periods of the week. But today, going to drama class just made me feel even more sad, because I couldn't stop thinking about how, once Lucinda was mayor, we'd never have it again.

Mrs. Cheng let Polly make an announcement before we got started. "Auditions for the fall musical are next week," Polly told us all. "We're doing *The Lion King*, and it's going to be super-fun. I hope all of you will at least consider trying out. It's going to have a big cast, so we need a lot of actors! Even if you don't want to perform, you should come anyway, and Mrs. Cheng will tell you about what we need for stage crew. If you're interested in designing costumes or building scenery or running lights and sound, then we need your involvement, too."

It was so dumb how Polly acted like this school play was so important when in fact it didn't matter outside of the four walls of Lawrenceville Middle School. Not like the election, which really *did* matter.

I couldn't understand how people could spend so much time on something so meaningless, then claim that they were too busy to spend their time on the things that were actually meaningful.

We need your involvement, Polly had said. No, you don't. Not as much as Janet needs people's involvement.

And just like that, all of a sudden, looking at Polly, I had an idea.

Mrs. Cheng divided us into small groups so we could each take a different fairy tale and adapt it for a modern-day setting. I wasn't in Polly's group. But as soon as everyone started talking and planning, I slipped away from my group, ran over to Polly's, and tapped her on the shoulder.

"Look, *Dahlina*," I said. "I know we don't always get along or whatever. But there's something really serious going on, and if we don't figure out what to do about it, then you and I are *both* going to be miserable."

Polly narrowed her eyes at me, like she couldn't tell if I was playing a prank on her or if I was actually crazy. "What on earth is this about?" she asked. "What do you want from me? We're supposed to be working on our skits right now, you know. Can't you ever just do things the way you're supposed to, Maddie?"

She was about to turn back to her small group, and I

could see Molly waiting for her cue to jump in and save her friend from having to talk to me, and Holly giving me the Holly Look, and Mrs. Cheng making her rounds through the room, about to notice that I was in the wrong place. So I just blurted it out.

The next mayor of Lawrenceville is going to get rid of all art in schools. No more drama class. No more school plays. No more Mrs. Cheng. There's somebody else running against her, and she wants us to keep arts education. But she's going to lose unless we help her.

Polly's eyes were as wide as saucers. "Are you kidding?" she demanded.

"I'm dead serious."

"Why would anyone want to do that to us?"

"Because she doesn't care about us," I said. "And because she can. Because she thinks no one's going to stop her."

"All right," Polly said decisively, and for the first time since Daniel semi-quit, I felt my heart lift. Because Polly sounded how I wanted to feel: confident. "I'm calling an emergency meeting at Jordan's tomorrow after school. I'll get people to show up if you come ready to tell us how we can fight back."

Mrs. Cheng noticed me then and said, "Maddie, is there a reason why you're not with your group?"

"Sorry, Mrs. Cheng!" I said. To Polly, I muttered, "I don't really hang out at Jordan's."

What I meant was, *I'm not really welcome at Jordan's.*

"Well," Polly said, "you do now."

CHAPTER 13

It seemed like half the seventh grade showed up at Jordan's Hot House for the next day's emergency meeting. Every beanbag chair had at least two kids squished onto it. Every booth was packed to the brim, with kids not only sitting six to a table but even more sitting on the tables themselves. I saw the drama kids and the band kids and the choir kids, the ones who made the literary magazine and the ones who made video games, the ballerinas and the painters and the poets.

I hadn't been to Jordan's since a birthday party three years ago—one of those parties where the birthday kid's parents insist on inviting everyone in the whole class—and somehow it had gotten *even cooler* since then.

So. Much. Soda!

Pizza!

JORDA

Skee-Ba

Giant Jenga!

Grown-ups refuse to hang out at Jordan's. Dad says it gives him a headache. Mom says she has nightmares set there. There is a small, noise-proof "retreat room" on the opposite side of the kitchen, where adults can sit quietly and check their phones while soft rock plays in the background.

I couldn't imagine how Polly might make our classmates pipe down long enough for me to tell them about the mayoral election. But then the piercing sound of an air horn blasted out. Some kids shrieked or clapped their hands over their ears, and we all turned in the direction of the noise.

It was coming from Polly—or, more specifically, from Polly's phone, which she'd hooked up to a speaker. She

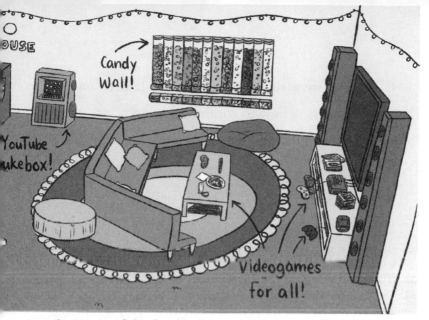

Candy Wall!

YouTube jukebox!

Videogames for all!

stood on top of the back of a booth, towering over everyone else.

The room fell silent as we all looked up at her. The car-racing video game was paused. The jukebox was shut off. All of Jordan's Hot House belonged to Polly—for the moment, at least.

We are here today to discuss an issue of utmost importance.

There's a threat that affects every single one of us. And only together can we fight it.

People were silent, enraptured. I had to hand it to Polly: She knew how to command a room.

"You've probably never heard of Lucinda Burghart before, but she is poised to become the new mayor of Lawrenceville. And if we let that happen, she is going to destroy our lives."

Polly started pointing to people one by one and telling them what Lucinda was going to do to them.

The room was a mix of horrified gasps, outraged *nos*, and stunned silence.

"*That* is what Lucinda is planning to do to us if she wins," Polly said. "Your own parents are probably planning to vote for her. *Most* adults are planning to vote for her. You know why? Because nobody cares what we think.

"*But*," Polly said, and I could feel the whole room hanging on her every word. Even *I* was leaning forward, eager to hear what came after *but*, what our hope might be, even though I *knew* our hope; I was the one who'd found it, after all.

"But," Polly repeated, "there is one other candidate in this race. Her name is Janet Teneman. She wants us to keep doing art and being creative. We can trust Janet. All we need to do is get her elected."

Isabelle raised her hand, like we were in school. "How can *we* get her elected when we can't even vote?" she asked.

"We can't vote," Polly said, "but that doesn't mean we're powerless. So Maddie's going to tell us how we can win. Maddie, come on up here."

The crowd parted to let me walk slowly to the front of the room. I climbed up on top of the booth so I was standing next to Polly.

But as soon as I made it there, it was like whatever spell she'd cast over the room was broken. People had been willing to listen to her. But they definitely weren't going to listen to me.

Uh-oh.

Now what was I going to do?

CHAPTER 14

"Hey!" I hollered. My voice was louder than I'd ever heard it before.

The grumbling of my classmates came to an abrupt halt.

"Look," I said, "Janet is *my* friend. I've known her since I was three years old. *I* found out what Lucinda was plotting. *I* asked Janet to run for mayor. *I* helped collect signatures so that Janet's name would appear on the ballot. And now *I* am going to tell you how we can win this thing.

"I don't care if you like me, but you should listen to me. Because this is *it*, guys. These are your only two options: Lucinda or Janet. And if we don't work together,

Lucinda is what we're going to get. Now, personally, I don't want Lucinda. Do you?"

"No," a bunch of people muttered.

Polly said, "We all know that not everyone in this room gets along. We want different things, we're in different clubs, we run in different circles. But for the next two months, between now and Election Day, we need to set all of that aside, because we need to win."

She looked straight at me as she said it, and I got her meaning perfectly: Just because we were working toward the same goal, that didn't make us friends.

Which was fine by me. I didn't want a friend like *Polly* anyway.

I just wanted to help Janet.

"Our only hope of winning is to run a really strong campaign," I announced. "Lucinda already has people working for her. But we have ourselves. Lucinda has already raised a lot of money. But we have *manpower*. We need to do everything Lucinda has done. And then we need to do *even more*."

"So what else does Lucinda have already?" Polly asked.

And I presented my list.

"That's everything I know for sure that Lucinda has already done for her campaign," I concluded.

"What about us?" asked Deke. "What have we done?"

"Nothing," I answered.

There was a moment of silence as everyone took in the enormity of the task ahead of us. Then Polly said, "So we'd better get started."

"For the slogan," Chloe spoke up, "it could say something about how Janet cares more about young people than Lucinda does."

"Like 'Kids for Janet'?" Molly suggested.

Chloe chewed on her bottom lip, and I could see her

playing around with different combinations of words in her brain. Chloe is the editor of *Fishsticks*, our school's literary magazine. "Something about how Janet's not just for selfish grown-ups; she's for everyone. Maybe 'Janet for all'? Or 'Janet for the future'?"

It all kind of sounded the same to me, but the rest of the creative writing kids seemed pleased by "Janet for the future," so that decided it.

"We'll need to print our slogan on yard signs," I said.

"I guess we can't just use, like, normal printer paper?" Deke asked.

"Not unless you want it to turn into pulp the next time it rains," Polly replied.

"My parents actually run a printing company," Molly volunteered. "They print logos on signs and banners and magnets and baseball caps and stuff like that."

An appreciative murmur went through the room.

"That's amazing!" I exclaimed. "Do you think they'd let us print all this stuff for free?"

Molly shook her head. "I've had them print materials before for my youth group, and they still need to charge a little bit of money to cover the cost of the supplies. But they'll give us a big discount."

"So no matter what, we need to raise at least a little money," I said.

"How?" asked Polly.

It was a good question.

"We could all chip in our allowances for the next two months," Lucas suggested.

Nicole nodded. "I would do that. I'd rather be two months further away from saving up for a trampoline than have the dance team taken away from me."

"I wouldn't do that," Holly objected.

Of course you wouldn't, I thought. Trust Holly's one sentence of the day to be something negative.

"Not everyone *gets* an allowance," Dylan pointed out.

"We can start by chipping in our own money," Nicole said. "Any amount that you can contribute will help, even if it's just a dime. And we can *also* fundraise outside of this room. So it's okay if *you* can't give any money, Holly. You can work on getting other people to donate instead. We can do bake sales, or sell the magnets and baseball caps at marked-up prices and make a profit from them."

Holly gave a Holly Look about this, but everyone else looked impressed.

"I ran the fundraiser for the dance team last year," Nicole explained. "We had to raise enough money for all new costumes. So that's how I know about that stuff."

"Could you be in charge of fundraising for the campaign, too?" I asked.

Nicole grinned. "Totally."

"Does Janet already have a website?" Isabelle asked. When I shook my head, she said, "Can Coding Club be in charge of making her one? We make awesome websites, but hardly anybody ever visits them. Last year we made this site that was a list of every first name we could think of, and barely any of you even *looked* at it." Isabelle gave a general glare to the room at large. "It's a *really* good website," she said, as if challenging any of us to deny it.

"You should definitely make Janet's website," I said. "I promise we'll all look at it."

Isabelle nodded, mollified, and then pulled out a laptop and propped it up against an arcade game, maybe so she could start coding right then and there.

"What do you guys think about this for a logo?" Theo asked, holding up his sketchbook.

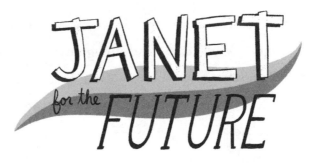

"Oooh!" we all said, and Theo nodded in satisfaction.

"Send that to me as a file," Isabelle told him briskly, "and I'll get it up on the website. Oh, the URL is JanetforLawrenceville.com, by the way. I just bought it. Nicole, you'll pay me back once we've raised some money, right?" She didn't wait for Nicole's response, though, and just went right back to typing on her computer.

"Can we meet Janet?" Evan asked me. "I've never met a politician before."

I almost laughed at the idea of Janet, *my* Janet, being called a politician—but then I realized that's exactly what she was now.

"I think so," I replied. "When?"

"Tomorrow," Polly suggested.

"Do you all *want* to come back here tomorrow?" I asked.

"Oh, yeah," Polly answered for everyone. "We are going to be here every day until the election. We're going to be here every day until the day we win."

"Janet for mayor!" someone shouted from the back. And then the rest of the room took up the cry.

CHAPTER 15

When Janet and I opened the door to Jordan's the next afternoon, we were greeted with so much screaming, you'd think that Janet was Taylor Swift paying a visit to the seventh graders of Lawrenceville.

I knew her first, guys!

Janet hadn't even been sure that she wanted to come meet all the kids.

"I thought you wanted a job," I reminded her.

"I did," she said. "I do. But . . . I don't know, do I want *this* job? Maybe I want to be an astronaut. Or a pastry chef. Or . . . something."

"I feel so embarrassed about the plagiarism scandal, I kind of just want to hide," she admitted. "I don't know. Running for mayor seemed like a fun thing to do, but then it got really serious, really fast."

"You're a hero to my entire school," I told her. "Being a hero is a fun thing to do."

"Can I still be a hero even if I'm not perfect?" she asked. "Even if I lose?"

"Of course," I told her. I hoped I was right about that. Janet was the only hero we had.

But now that we were at the front of the room full of cheering seventh graders, Janet seemed transformed. She was all confidence and energy, just like a politician should be. "Thank you so much!" Janet shouted. "Thank you! I'm so excited to be running for mayor, and I'm honored to have all of your support.

"You guys are amazing. When I was at Lawrenceville Middle School, I was president of the Weather Club, but that was about it. I wasn't doing anything as meaningful as you are. I thought politics was a boring thing that only affected grown-ups and that only adults could be involved in. I am so impressed that you've all figured out—years earlier than I did—that what happens in politics makes a difference to *all* of us, so we can *all* be political activists.

"I can't promise you that we will win, but I can promise you that we will give it everything we've got. And whether or not we win, we are going to make a positive impact on this city. Who's with me?"

Everyone cheered again. I felt like I was going to burst with pride.

But then the crowd broke up to get to work, and I started feeling kind of . . . lonely. Kids kept coming up to Janet to talk to her. They seemed fascinated by everything she had to say, which made sense, because she's interesting and also now an important politician. And she seemed fascinated by what *they* had to say, which also made sense, because Janet is an excellent listener and very supportive.

But it made me feel jealous and unnecessary. The way Janet was looking at them, focused on everything they were saying, nodding and asking thoughtful questions— that's how she'd always treated *me*. Me and nobody else, because she was *my* babysitter.

Only now it seemed like I wasn't so special after all.

Yesterday it had felt like my classmates needed me, because I had a solution to their problems. But now that I'd delivered that solution, none of *them* seemed to need me anymore, either.

Nobody seemed to notice when I went outside. I sat down on a bench and pulled out my sketch pad. The air smelled crisp and autumnal. I wondered if there was a name for this sort of weather. I'd ask Janet if I ever got her to myself again.

The garbage collector pulled up and started loading trash bags from the Jordan's dumpster into his truck. His keys came unclipped from his belt as he was reaching for the last of the bags, so I picked them up and handed them back to him.

"Hmph. I have no idea," said the garbage collector.

"You should vote for Janet Teneman," I told him.

"Look, I don't have any time to figure out who to vote for," the man said. "I might not even have time to vote. The sanitation department is understaffed, and I'm doing the work of two men here. This cesspool of children, Jordan's? This isn't even supposed to be on my route. They keep expanding my territory. It's ridiculous—no one can fit in this many stops in a day. I could be the greatest garbage man of all time, and I still wouldn't be able to handle this."

"Okay," I said, "but if you do vote, will you vote for Janet?"

"Why should I?" the garbage man asked.

"Because she's going to make sure there continues to be funding for arts education in public schools," I answered promptly.

"And why would I care about *that*?" he asked.

"BECAUSE I SAID SO!" I wanted to yell at him, but I didn't, because Dad says that's not a convincing argument, and anyway, it's rude to yell at strangers.

"I'm not in public school," the garbage man said. "I'm

not an artist. Maybe I would be, if I wasn't working all the time. Hah! That'll never happen."

"Okay," I said. "Okay, I get it."

"Kids!" the garbage collector muttered under his breath as he headed off.

I went back inside.

I was going to ask Janet what she thought about hiring more employees for the sanitation department so that the people who worked there would have more time off, but she was still surrounded by her crowd of admirers, so I didn't bother. Instead I just wrote "Hire more garbage collectors?" on a blank page in my sketch pad and stomped over to My Friend Daniel.

Wow, I've done so much important stuff for the campaign that I am <u>starving</u>.

Important stuff like what?

Um...

"What if not enough people care about art in public schools?" I asked Daniel.

"Why wouldn't they?" Daniel asked, his mouth full of pizza.

"Because," I said, "a lot of people only care about issues that directly affect them. Artsy kids care about arts in schools. Garbage collectors care about garbage. People who drive cars care about potholes." I sighed. "How do you make people care about issues that don't directly affect them?"

"You don't care about stuff that doesn't directly affect you," My Friend Daniel told me.

I frowned at him. "Sure I do."

"No, you don't. That's why you don't care about potholes, whatever those are. Because they have nothing to do with you."

"Yeah, okay," I muttered. "Name one thing you care about that doesn't have to do with you."

Daniel shrugged. "Nah. I only care about things in my own life. But I don't feel bad about it. Lots of people only care about their own stuff." He looked around the room. "Not Janet, though."

"How do you know?" I asked.

"Because," he said, rolling his eyes at me, "she's running for mayor just so kids can have art class. And she's not even a kid."

"You're right," I said, feeling a swell of pride for Janet even as I felt a swell of sadness that I was losing her to everyone else. "She cares a lot about other people's stuff. I think that's why she'd be a good mayor."

Now, how were we going to convince the rest of the world?

CHAPTER 16

Within a week, Jordan's Hot House had been transformed into Janet for Mayor campaign headquarters. Along with every other artistic kid at Lawrenceville Middle School, I spent hours there every day after school, working to get Janet elected.

Everyone helped one another out, but different people quickly took charge of specific aspects of the campaign.

$5 for a magnet, $15 for a hat, and $35 for a shirt.

Every penny goes toward helping Janet win!

QUEEN OF MERCH: MOLLY!

That's what Jordan's Hot House was like now. If we got hungry from working too hard, there was always the candy wall. If we got tired from working too hard, there were always the beanbag chairs. And if we just couldn't work anymore, there were always video games.

Everyone was in charge of something specific and important. Except for me. Mostly I helped out everyone else, and I answered a lot of questions. All the kids asked me for permission before they made any big decisions. Which was funny, because I didn't know any more about running a political campaign than they did.

It wasn't just at Jordan's that people had questions for me. It was at school, too. All of a sudden, kids who'd never wanted to talk to me kept approaching me at

lunch or in the locker room or between classes to ask
me for things.

"If Janet wins, can she..."

...make my dad's boss pay him more money? He works ALL THE TIME, and we're still broke.

...fix the ramp so I can get down to the lake? My mom makes a big scene every time we go there. It's really embarrassing.

...stop people from smoking in parks? It gives me asthma attacks.

...run a bus from school to downtown? It takes a long time to walk and gets really cold in the winter.

...get new books in the library? I've read like every one there, and the librarian says she doesn't have the budget to get more.

...make a law that you have to wear a helmet when you ride a bike? My dad never does. If he won't listen to me, he'll at least listen to the law.

"I hope so," I told everyone who asked me, and I wrote all their requests down on my sketchpad. I wanted to say yes, because I wanted to help them, and because I wanted them to join Janet's campaign. But I didn't actually know if Janet *could* do all of this. Did mayors control how much bosses paid their employees, or bus routes, or library budgets? And was there some *reason* why the current mayor hadn't already done these things? They sounded like good ideas to me. But maybe there was some secret reason why they were *bad* ideas, and I didn't even know it, and that's why they hadn't already happened.

Could a mayor do even bigger things? Could she stop the use of fossil fuels, like Mr. Okereke wanted? Could she declare war? Could she save an endangered species? Could she send people to jail for calling other people weird?

It suddenly occurred to me that, even though we were running for mayor, I didn't a hundred percent actually know what the mayor did.

I didn't want to ask Mr. Valdez, even though he was the social studies teacher, because I assumed he'd say something like . . .

But when I finally asked him, what he actually said was, "That's a great question, Maddie."

Can you believe it?! I, Maddie Polansky, asked a great question! In school! Give me straight As and let me graduate forever, because clearly I have mastered this school thing today, and it's only going to go downhill from here.

"America is designed to have a system of checks and balances," he said. "That means that different parts of the government limit one another's power. If we lived in a monarchy, then the king or queen could just do whatever they wanted, whenever they wanted. They could outlaw anything, or require anything, and no one could stop them."

"But because we live in a democracy," Mr. Valdez explained, "nobody has that sort of absolute power. Decisions are divided up among the lawmakers, the courts, and the executive branch—that's the mayor. Other decisions are divided up between the national government, the state government, and the city government. And if any one part of the government oversteps its boundaries, then it's up to the other parts to stop it."

That made sense in principle. Even if she *did* get elected, Janet couldn't just do whatever she felt like. But it still didn't tell me whether Janet could do any of the specific things that the kids in school kept asking me about.

"Ugh, this is so easy," Polly said when I mentioned that I was worried about this. "Just tell everyone that Janet will do exactly what they want, and then they'll all support her."

"Yeah, but what if that's a lie?" I asked. "What if she gets elected, and then it turns out she can't do any of these things after all because of checks and balances?"

"Well, by then it'll be too late." Polly flipped her hair. "She'll already be the mayor, and even if they're disappointed, there won't be anything they can do about it."

I thought about my mom telling me that politicians sometimes made campaign promises and then didn't stick to them when they actually took office. I didn't see any difference between that and just outright *lying.*

"Lots of people lie, or at least pretend to be something they're not, in order to get people to like them," Polly told me, exasperated. "It's not a big deal."

Maybe that's why people don't like me. I'm no good at pretending.

CHAPTER 17

"I'm so nervous," My Friend Daniel said, hopping from foot to foot. "I'm so nervous I'm so nervous I'm so—"

"*Stop* it," I said. "You're being annoying, and you're making *me* nervous."

We were at the park, close to the farmers market, about to kick off Janet's very first campaign rally. Everything *looked* good, but looks could be deceiving.

All of us had brought along parents, grandparents, or other potential Janet voters. I saw a bunch of people I recognized from the farmers market, like Mr. Okereke, the man with the climate change petition. Holly was selling T-shirts and bumper stickers to everyone who came

by. Polly was going over Janet's speech with her one last time. Dylan was recording everything, while Chloe was hunched over her phone, posting constant updates to social media. And everyone had questions for me.

"Are there any more sign-up forms?" asked Deke.

"Where's the band supposed to set up?" asked Lucas.

"Is there a chair for my grandpa?" asked Nicole.

"In my bag, by the flagpole, and just take Molly's," I answered.

"Who's Molly?" Nicole said.

"You know what I mean. Adrianne."

Nicole gave me a weird look and then they all ran back to work.

I wrote "Put more benches in the park so people can sit down" on my notepad.

"I'm so proud to see how hard all you kids are working on this campaign," Mom said, placing her hand on my shoulder. "What a terrific hobby Janet has found for you! She is just the greatest babysitter, isn't she?"

Okay, first of all? In no way was this campaign Janet's idea. Second of all, a *hobby*?!

"She's a great babysitter," Dad agreed, "but we'll have to find a new one if she wins! I was just talking to some folks over there—I'm pretty sure one of them was a statistician, and she said Janet has a one in three chance of getting elected!"

Translation: Dad had talked to some people at this rally; maybe they had jobs, but definitely not anything involving statistics; and Janet had a one in a million chance of getting elected.

Great.

"I hope this event gets started, because I have to leave pretty soon," Mom said, checking her watch. "It's week two of my ten-week class for parents on how to support your children in their passions, and I don't want to be late."

I took that as my cue, and I hollered, "Lucas! Let's do it!" And with that, the rally began.

The band kicked things off by playing "America the Beautiful," because it sounded political, and then "Call Me Maybe," because they knew it really well and didn't have time to learn new music. Even more people gathered around to hear them play.

Next, Mr. Xian gave a speech about how important arts education was. Then it was Janet's turn to talk.

"Thank you to everyone who came out to support me on this beautiful fall day," she said. "My name is Janet Teneman, and I am running for mayor!"

Everyone in the park burst into applause.

"I'm here to support the future of Lawrenceville," Janet said. "I grew up here, and I love this town. I love the people here, and the parks, and the architecture, and the *weather*! I think Lawrenceville has the ideal ratio of cloudy to sunny days, don't you?"

There was some scattered applause, like people wanted to support Janet even though they weren't totally sure how many cloudy days was ideal. I saw Polly mouthing words to Janet, and I guessed that the weather wasn't supposed to be part of her speech.

"This town is great," Janet went on, getting back on track. "But my opponent wants to make it worse. We're a diverse place with a lot of creative, motivated citizens. Think about the talented band you just heard. Look at that beautiful banner. Watch the amazing videos that are on my campaign website. Our schools are offering students the education and the support to create all of this and more."

I saw Mr. Xian nodding. He looked proud.

"If my opponent gets elected, none of those skills will be encouraged anymore. Students will be taught exactly what's on standardized tests and nothing else. But if you take anything away from this rally, I hope it's that the kids of Lawrenceville are so much more than just test-takers and bubble-fillers. They are whole individuals with specific passions and knowledge and curiosity. And they deserve an education that treats them as the complete and distinct human beings that they are."

Everyone applauded—not just the kids but the adults, too. I felt a warm swell of pride. But then I saw Mr. Okereke shaking his head.

"What?" I asked him.

"It's not enough, kid," he told me. "She can't win on that."

"What do you mean?"

"A political campaign can't just run on maintaining the status quo. It's got to run on *progress*."

"Huh?" I was annoyed. Janet was giving a great speech. This was a great rally. And Mr. Okereke was ruining it with his bad attitude.

"Right now, all your girl is saying is that she won't make things any worse," he explained. "She's promising to keep things the same. That's the status quo. And it's not what makes voters turn out. She has to convince us that she's going to *improve* our situation. What's more motivating: *Fear* that Lucinda will make our lives worse? Or *hope* that Janet will make our lives better?"

FEAR　　　　HOPE

I had no idea. All I heard was Mr. Okereke telling me
that protecting arts education for students wasn't enough.

Which was basically what the garbage man had
said, too.

It was what a lot of people had said. That this thing,
which was life-or-death for me and all the rest of the kids
here, didn't matter to them at all.

"Do you think that people only care about issues that
affect them directly?" I asked Mr. Okereke.

"That's true for some folks," he said. "But not
everyone. I care about the planet, remember, even though
by the time climate change has progressed far enough

that Lawrenceville becomes unlivable, I'll be long gone. I'm not trying to save it for myself.

"You can't fight exclusively for things that make your *own* life better, know what I mean? That's selfish and small-minded. Do not ever value the quality of your life over the quality of everyone else's. You're no more important than any other human being out there. Instead, you've got to fight for a better *society*, a society in which *everyone* can have access to a better life."

I looked at him.

"Sorry," he said. "When I'm not out here getting signatures for my petition, I'm a professor of political science at the college."

"I bet your class is really hard," I told him.

He laughed.

Lucas was getting the band back into position so they could play another song. (Specifically, they were going to play "Call Me Maybe" again, because they really didn't know that many songs.) But I put up my hand to stop him as I walked up to the front of the crowd, where Janet was finishing her speech.

"We need to think bigger," I told her, and I gave her my notepad.

Janet took a quick look at it. Then she gave me a big smile.

"Is that what you meant?" I asked Mr. Okereke.

"Yeah, kid," he said with a grin and a slow nod. "That'll do it."

CHAPTER 18

THE LAWRENCEVILLE GAZETTE

ONE MONTH REMAINS IN RACE FOR MAYOR

After a quiet start, newcomer Janet Teneman's campaign for mayor of Lawrenceville is picking up momentum. A series of well-attended rallies have expanded her base, and she has put together a coalition of supporters with a broad range of backgrounds.

"Janet says she's going to hire more guys for waste management," said longtime sanitation department employee Martin Gregory, age sixty-two. "That's enough to get my vote, because do you even know how many hours a day I have to work? It's crazy. Honestly, why am I even talking to you right now when I still have so much garbage to collect today? I have to go."

"I've never voted before," said Pedro Hernández, a twenty-one-year-old student, "but I'm going to vote for Janet because I think it's cool that she's basically my age and she's already running for office. I met her at an event last week. She really listened to me."

For other voters, however, Teneman's youth is more of a hindrance than an asset. "She's inexperienced," said Rhianna Binkot, a real estate agent, age forty-five. "Lucinda Burghart has been working in city government for years. Sure, she's not perfect, but she's a known quantity, and I trust her."

Although Teneman is gaining ground, Burghart is still polling significantly ahead. "We don't need to talk about Janet," said Burghart's campaign manager, Richard Langston, who has run many local and statewide political campaigns in years past. "She's a distraction, nothing more. The real story here is all the money that Lucinda Burghart is going to save the taxpayers of Lawrenceville."

The two candidates will go head-to-head for the first time at a debate, sponsored by the League of Women Voters, at 6:00 p.m. on Thursday.

We did a lot of practicing with Janet before the debate. Molly was on the forensics team, so she pretended to be Lucinda, and Janet practiced rebutting her. We watched lots of old presidential debates on the giant screen at Jordan's for inspiration. And we kept a dodgeball at Jordan's that anyone could throw at Janet at any time while asking a debate question, which Janet would have to answer as soon as she caught it.

When the day of the debate arrived, we were so excited that we all showed up early to the auditorium. The atmosphere was electric and hyper, but once we tried to enter the auditorium, it took a steep nosedive.

There were a lot of shocked gasps and grumbling. "That's not fair!" someone yelled.

"Why can't the kids come in to watch the debate?" Janet asked.

The security guard didn't smile or look apologetic as he replied, "Because there's limited seating inside, and the priority is to get voters in there. Furthermore, the children might be noisy. We need to make sure the audience is able to hear the candidates."

"I *am* a candidate," Janet told him, looking annoyed.

"We can be really quiet!" Polly shouted, and to prove it we all went perfectly silent.

But the security guard did not seem impressed. "I don't make the rules," he said.

"So who does?" Janet asked.

He shrugged.

"See, this is why *Janet* should make the rules," I whispered to Daniel.

"But they came all this way," Janet tried. "I wouldn't be here at all if it weren't for them."

"If you want to take it up with the organizers, go ahead," he said. "I'm just doing my job."

Janet went around to the back of the building, I guess to talk to some people about getting us in, while we stood in a huddle and waited. She came back to us a few minutes later looking pale. "The rules do say that nobody under eighteen is allowed in," she said. "And guess who made the rules?"

"Who?" we asked.

"The city council," she said grimly.

It took a moment before I realized: "Lucinda's *on* the city council!"

"But that's cheating!" My Friend Daniel exclaimed. "She's keeping us out on purpose!"

Janet ran a hand through her hair. She looked utterly lost.

Polly spoke up. "It's okay, Janet," she said. "We're not mad at *you*. We can wait outside and listen to the debate online."

We all nodded reluctantly. We'd been looking forward to watching Janet debate. We'd been excited to cheer her on, and a lot of kids had wanted to see the evil Lucinda in person for the first time. My Friend Daniel had literally been rehearsing the mean look he was going to give her during the whole debate.

But Polly was right that this wasn't Janet's fault, and if we kept being angry about it, we'd just make Janet feel guilty.

So we all agreed that it was fine. "We'll be cheering you on out here," Michaela said.

"You've got this in the bag," Theo added.

Janet still looked sick, though.

I pulled her aside. "What's going on?" I asked.

"I'm *scared*!" she blurted out—but in a whisper, so no one else could hear.

I thought back to how nervous I'd felt when I had asked Lucinda that one question at the town hall. I got why Janet would feel scared. "But you're so good at speaking in front of crowds," I reassured her. "You've been doing tons of rallies and fundraisers, and everyone loves you."

"Yes," she said, "but that's different. Everyone goes to those to listen to me, not to argue with me. Those rallies are filled with my supporters, but the audience for this debate is going to include a lot of people who want to see me lose. They want to see Lucinda make a fool of me. And I'll be in there all alone!"

"You won't be *all* alone," I tried to reassure her. "Your parents will be in the audience, right? And your friends?"

"But none of *you* will be there." Janet gestured to all of us kids. "And you're the ones who really believe that I can win."

Janet was spiraling. She was sweaty and shaky, and if I didn't do something fast, she was going to work herself into such a state of nerves that Lucinda would be able to beat her without even trying.

"Janet," I said with more confidence than I felt, "you've practiced so much for this. You're ready. Whenever the moderator asks you a question, just imagine that it's one of us tossing you the dodgeball. Just answer it like you're talking to us."

"I don't know if I can do it," she said, knotting her fingers together.

I didn't know if she meant that she couldn't debate or couldn't be mayor, but either way, I *knew* that her doubts were unfounded. "You're smart and a good listener," I told her. "People open up to you and want to tell you their problems. And you genuinely *care* about their problems, and you work to help fix them. You have good ideas, but you're open to everyone else's good ideas, too. Most people aren't like that, Janet."

It's true that she was usually a good listener, but in that moment she didn't seem to be listening to me at all.

It was like she'd locked herself into her own little closet of stage fright and nobody could reach her in there.

I checked the time. "The debate starts in twenty minutes," I said. "You should go."

Janet nodded numbly and staggered inside. I watched her go.

"I need to get into that debate," I whispered to myself. But how?

CHAPTER 19

I refused to let Lucinda's biased rules stand in my way—or in Janet's. I was going in there whether I was allowed to or not.

I watched the crowd of adults who were waiting to get into the auditorium for the debate, and then, when I felt as ready as I could, I slipped into line with them. I tried to blend in, which is hard to do when you're a foot shorter than everyone else. I watched the security guard quickly check the bags of the people who were in line in front of me, then wave them through.

When I got to the front of the line, he said, "Sorry, no kids allowed inside."

But this time I was ready. I stood up straight and pretended to be like Lucinda—someone who believed she was always right; someone who believed she always deserved to get her way. "My aunt told me you might say that," I replied coolly, "and she said you had instructions to make an exception for me."

"Do I?" he said. "Who's your aunt?"

"She's running for mayor," I went on, "and she's on the city council. She made the rule that no children are allowed at the debate, which makes sense, because children are usually so noisy and disrespectful. But she wants *me* there. She said she'd given you special instructions about it. Didn't you get them?"

The security guard scratched his neck.

"*Don't* tell me I need to call my aunt about this," I said. "The debate starts in just a few minutes, and she'll be extremely annoyed if she has to interrupt her pre-debate meditation ritual just to come let me in. You know, this is the same ritual she's been using since she was in *the Olympics*."

He let out a big breath. "It's just you, right? You don't have a crew of friends who you're going to try to bring in with you?"

I gave him my best withering look. "Of course not. Like I said, other children are *so* noisy."

And he stood aside and let me in.

Yes!

I darted down the hall, weaving my way around the slower-walking adults, and found a seat a few rows back from the stage—close enough that I could see, but hopefully not so close that Lucinda would notice me.

A few minutes later, the moderator silenced the room so she could get started.

A big round of applause greeted them as they took the stage. Lucinda looked confident and a little bored. Janet was wide-eyed and terrified.

Genesis said, "Let's get started with a broad question: Why do you think that you would be a good mayor for Lawrenceville? Ms. Burghart, please start us off."

Lucinda grinned like a crocodile. "Let me start by thanking the League of Women Voters for hosting us. And thank you to Genesis, of course—always a pleasure to speak with you. And enormous thanks to everyone in the audience, and those listening at home, for taking the time out of your busy lives to think about the future of our city." She paused, then added begrudgingly, "And of course, thank you to my opponent for being here."

I rolled my eyes.

"I am the right pick for Lawrenceville because I have many years of experience. I know how this city runs, and I know how to get things done. I have the best interests of Lawrenceville taxpayers in mind at all times. I'm going to cut government funding for all sorts of unnecessary city services, which means I'm going to save money for everyone in this room. Now, many people don't know this about me, but I am in fact an Olympian."

"And as an Olympian," she went on, "I understand self-reliance, hard work, and constant improvement. That is what I'll bring to this city. Thank you."

Everyone around me cheered, even though Genesis Lee asked them to hold their applause until the end. And then it was Janet's turn.

I winced. Janet was gripping the podium and breathing funny.

"I grew up here?" Janet went on. "I . . . want to help people?"

The crowd was growing restless. The couple sitting next to me was whispering and giggling.

"Do you need to take a break, honey?" Lucinda asked Janet with a sickly sweet concern. She put on a baby voice to say, "I know your first debate can be vewy scawy!"

Ugh!

I stood up and made eye contact with Janet. Her gaze settled on me, and her mouth opened in a little o of surprise. I mimed tossing her a dodgeball, and her face relaxed into a smile. She mimed catching it.

This did not go unnoticed by Lucinda. "What is this?" she snapped. "Will somebody please escort this little girl from the audience?"

All these people are staring at me.

"We have rules here for a reason," Lucinda went on, her face flushed. "Children are disruptive, as you can clearly see. They are not members of the electorate—they can't vote, and this process is reserved for all of us who can."

"You know what?" Janet spoke up loudly. "The reason why I should be mayor is because I fundamentally disagree with what Lucinda just said."

The audience fell silent again, and Janet went on, her voice strong now. "My opponent treats some people like they matter more than others. She seems to think adults matter more than children, and rich adults who can vote matter most of all. I disagree. We are all people, and all of us are equally entitled to respect and opportunities.

"I originally got into this race because Lucinda intends to cut funding for arts education in schools. And while that may save some people some money, it will cost other people their happiness, their purpose, their future. And the people who will lose out? They don't have any power. They don't have a say. So I'm here to fight for them."

She meant *me*. Me and all the other kids gathered outside. I pictured them listening on their phones and cheering, and I wished we could all be in one place, cheering together.

Janet went on. "People open up to me. They always have, and they've been doing so more and more since I started this campaign. They tell me their problems, because they know that I *care* about them and that I'm going to work to make their lives better.

"Everyone in this audience has good ideas for improving Lawrenceville. You want this city to be more handicap-accessible. You want it to be easier to recycle and compost. You want a library that's not stuck in 2005. You want better buses and bike lanes and roads, so you can get around. I want to hear *all* your ideas and *all* your concerns. Even—*especially*—if you don't have any power. And *that* is why I'd be a good mayor."

I could barely hear the moderator telling the audience members to be quiet over the sound of their applause. Janet winked at me. I winked back at her. That was exactly what I'd told Janet was special about her! She'd heard me after all!

Lucinda's face was bright pink. "Oh, really?" she finally got out. "How exactly are you going to pay for all these pie-in-the-sky ideas? City buses and recycling programs don't fund themselves. You know who *does* fund them? The taxpayers! The very people here in this room!

Who are already giving up *quite* enough of their hard-earned dollars to the government, thank you very much!"

"Here's how," Janet said. "I'm going to bring more businesses into Lawrenceville. The new businesses will pay city taxes, and *that's* how we're going to afford all these programs. Because you know what?" She looked out at the audience, calm and clear. "There *should* be more businesses in Lawrenceville. There should be more employment opportunities here. I got good grades and graduated from college, yet my best hope of finding work in this town is becoming the *mayor*. It shouldn't be like that. There should be enough jobs in this town for everyone who wants to work!"

Wow. I was so proud of Janet, I thought I might burst.

"Next question," the moderator said once the applause had quieted down. "Ms. Teneman, you were accused of cheating when you were a student at Lawrenceville High School. Ms. Burghart has been quoted as saying, 'Once a cheater, always a cheater.' How do you respond to that? What would you say to someone who is reluctant to vote for you because of your history?"

Lucinda nodded firmly a number of times and raised

her eyebrows at the crowd like, *No way she's gonna be able to talk her way out of this one, folks!*

Fortunately, we had practiced this question. Janet shot me a smile, and I could tell she remembered what we'd discussed.

"When I was fourteen years old, I plagiarized an essay for English class," Janet said. "As a result, I failed the class and made it up in summer school. I was suspended. I wrote a letter of apology to my teacher. I made a bad choice, and I deserved to be disciplined for it.

"I learned a lot from that experience, and I have never cheated at anything again, because I've never forgotten the shame of it. One of the things I learned is this: *People can change.* If you let someone get away with bad behavior, they won't change. But if you hold them responsible for it—if you can get them to understand what they did wrong and why and how to do it differently—then they *can* change and grow and improve. I did."

The couple next to me, who'd been giggling before, was nodding thoughtfully now. I slipped them both "Janet for Mayor" buttons, and they grinned and took them.

"Ms. Burghart, your response?" the moderator said.

Lucinda was already shaking her head so hard I

THINGS I'LL BE FOREVER

An artist

A bad speller

definitely weird
~~definatly wierd~~

A dog lover

A strawberry hater

A person who watches every single superhero movie in theaters

thought it might fall off. "No," she said. "People don't change. My opponent is the same lazy girl who takes the easy way out because she doesn't want to actually do the work. She said herself that she hasn't even held down a proper job since she graduated! And I am the same goal-oriented straight shooter that I was when I competed in the Olympics."

I thought that the way Lucinda had made her point was nasty and rude, but I also thought that maybe both she *and* Janet were a little bit right. There were some parts of me that I couldn't imagine ever changing, qualities that were so much a part of *me* that I wouldn't want them to change even if they could.

But there were some ways in which I was already different from the Maddie I'd been just a few weeks ago. Today I felt like I was part of a community, like I was excited to reunite with the rest of the kids and talk about the debate with them and figure out what our next steps were. Today I felt like someone who mattered, someone who people relied on. Janet had always been there for me, to cook for me and drive me around and be my paid friend, but today, in her time of need, *I* was here for *her*.

So I thought that Janet had a point. People *could* change and grow and improve. Maybe I already had.

CHAPTER 20

After the debate, I wanted to talk to Janet right away and tell her what a good job she had done, but she was surrounded by a crowd of people congratulating her or asking her to do certain things if she became mayor. I stayed out of the way, because I didn't want to get between Janet and anyone who could vote for her.

When most of them had moved on, I started to approach Janet, but then another guy swooped in.

"Great work up there tonight," he said to her. "I wanted to introduce myself. My name is Chris Prince, and I'm a political strategist."

Janet shook his hand. "Good to meet you."

"I ran Enrique Peñate's reelection campaign a few

years ago," Chris told her, "as well as Governor Tuchman's. I was on staff for Senator Bradley's campaign as well."

"Wow," Janet said.

"I have to say, I'm not a fan of Burghart's policies," Chris went on. "I was disappointed when it looked like no one was going to challenge her, so I'm glad that you entered the race. And I've been impressed by the job you're doing, especially for a first-time candidate. You've really got people paying attention. And I suspect you're going to have a lot of new fans after your performance in this debate."

This dude knows what he's talking about!

"Thanks," Janet said.

"Listen," he said, "I don't want to overstep here, but I'd love to talk to you about managing your campaign."

"*You* want to manage my campaign?" Janet said, sounding flattered.

He nodded seriously. "I think you stand a chance, but it's an uphill battle, and you're only going to win with the right strategy. I hear that you've been running your campaign out of a children's restaurant with an all-volunteer team. But this is the big leagues, and it's time to get serious. If I came onboard, I'd suggest hiring at least one other full-time staff member and renting office space. I know it would require a bigger budget, but I have a lot of ideas for donors you haven't tapped into yet."

I walked away. I'd heard enough.

This guy, Chris Prince, was a political pro. He wanted to come in and help Janet beat Lucinda. And he seemed like he could actually make it happen. He had the experience, the connections, the confidence. He was exactly the sort of resource we needed on our side.

And yet I wished he'd just disappear.

I walked outside to where the rest of the kids were

dancing around, holding up "Janet for Mayor" signs, passing out stickers, and getting contact information from everyone who was coming out of the auditorium.

"Yay!" I said, plastering a smile on my face. "Sounds great!"

But all I could think of was that soon Chris would be in charge of all of this. All the questions and compliments and updates would go to him, not me. And that should have been a *good* thing, because he knew what to do with all of it, and I didn't.

After all, I reminded myself, winning was the most

important thing, and Chris knew how to win a political campaign. He'd done it before. Winning was what mattered, I told myself, so who cared how we got there?

Still, I felt sad. And dumb. I'd *just* started feeling useful to Janet, to the campaign, to the city and all the kids in it. I'd felt like people needed me for a little while, and it had been a good feeling.

But now I was realizing that had all been in my mind. Nobody really needed me. Not even Janet.

We celebrated for a long time outside the auditorium, and I kept wishing everyone would stop so I could go home. Janet had done really well in the debate—everyone agreed—but I was exhausted from trying to act happy about it when really, selfishly, I mostly just felt bad for myself.

I texted my parents to ask them to get me, but my mom was at a retreat about "intuitive parenting," and my dad had somehow turned off the electricity in our house and was trying to figure out how to turn it back on, so they both told me to just wait for Janet to be ready to leave.

Finally, the other kids left, and Janet finished talking to all her fans. "It's that time, Mads," she said to me, and we got in her car and headed toward home. Janet talked almost the whole way while I aimlessly drew circles in my notebook. "What an amazing event," she kept saying. "Wow. We prepared so well for that! I had an answer ready for almost every question she asked. Not the one about Mayor Peñate's new zoning restrictions. I don't know much about that, and Lucinda knows a lot. I'm going to have to study up on it. But everything else, right? The room literally broke into applause when I talked about my plan to open up a community center. They didn't clap that hard for anything Lucinda said."

"Yeah," I said, shading in one of my circles so it would look 3-D.

Janet glanced over at me, her forehead furrowed. "What did you think?" she asked me.

"You did great," I replied honestly.

"Do you think we got new voters out of it?"

"Yup," I said. "You got a ton of new supporters tonight." And then I couldn't help but add, "Especially Chris Prince."

"Oh, yeah," Janet agreed. "That was so cool. To have this big-deal political strategist compliment me and say he thinks I stand a chance! I just Googled him, and he's been around in local and state politics for ages. He's the real deal."

"He sure is," I agreed. I wished I didn't feel so rotten and jealous and small inside.

What I feel like right now.

Janet wanted to win. I wanted her to win. Our city would be better if she won. I needed to get over myself and be supportive of anyone and anything that could make that happen. "Where do you think he'll move your campaign headquarters to?" I asked casually.

"What?"

"I just figured, he's a campaign expert, so he's probably not going to run yours out of a—what would you call Jordan's?—a 'children's restaurant.'"

"Oh." Janet stopped at a red light and looked at me. "He's not moving my headquarters anywhere. He can't. Because he's not in charge of my campaign."

"Not *yet*," I corrected her.

She shook her head. "Chris offered to take over as campaign manager, and I told him I was honored, but I already had the best campaign manager I could want."

"But Janet . . ." I said. "I can't run a campaign. I'm no good at any of that stuff, and I don't know anything about politics."

Janet laughed. "What do you think you've been doing for the past six weeks? You collected signatures, you got me on the ballot, you recruited dozens of volunteers, you set up voter outreach efforts, you organized rallies, you talked to citizens to find out what they care about, you helped me figure out my platform, and you got me through this debate when I thought I was going to have a panic attack. You're my campaign manager, and you're a heck of a good one. No way am I letting you quit now."

"Really?" I said, a big grin creeping across my face.

"Really." Janet pulled into my driveway. I could see lights on in the kitchen and on the front porch, which meant that my dad must have figured out how to turn the electricity back on somehow. Our house looked bright and welcoming, and I felt bright, too.

"See you tomorrow, campaign manager?" Janet said as I got out of the car.

"See you tomorrow," I said, and I gave her a big smile.

CHAPTER 21

THE LAWRENCEVILLE GAZETTE

MAYOR'S RACE GROWS CLOSER AS FINAL COUNTDOWN TO ELECTION DAY BEGINS

With eighteen days left before the election, the race for mayor has grown increasingly competitive. The most recent poll shows that if the election were to be held tomorrow, 40 percent of voters would support political newcomer Janet Teneman.

"I never saw this coming," remarked Shaun Phillips, who served on the city council for two terms with Ms.

Burghart. "If you'd asked me a couple of months ago, I would have said Lu was a shoo-in. But now I'm seeing Janet Teneman's name everywhere. Every street I drive down, there's a 'Janet for Mayor' sign in someone's yard. Every time I bring in the mail, there's a handwritten postcard from one of Janet's supporters."

"Lucinda's campaign certainly has a lot working in its favor," commented longtime political strategist Chris Prince, who is not affiliated with either campaign. "She has name recognition. She has wealthy corporate donors, which means she has a significant amount of money to spend on advertising. She has hired a professional staff of experienced campaign organizers.

"But what she lacks—and what Janet has in spades— is ground support. Lucinda has far, far fewer volunteers, and those she has are giving far less of their time and energy. And no amount of money can buy that kind of authentic, self-motivated support."

Still, many voters remain undecided, while others have no plans to vote at all. "I don't pay enough attention to politics to know who to vote for," said Lena Fawkes, owner of Lena's Sweet Treats Cafe. "I'm going to leave that decision to the people who really care about it."

"The issue I'll base my decision on is housing security," said Steve Kopowski, who works in a call center. "I've been homeless on and off for many years. I've lived in shelters and low-income housing, I've crashed with family, and sometimes I've slept on the streets. I want to elect a mayor who's actually going to fix the homelessness problem in Lawrenceville. Both candidates promise to do something about it, but which of them is really going to make it a priority? Which of them will actually make a positive difference?"

In the last election for mayor, 23 percent of registered voters cast ballots. Both Burghart and Teneman are working to increase turnout this year. And indeed, the more competitive this race becomes, the more voters say they intend to come out and vote. Whether those intentions become reality or not, we will find out on November 8.

We were supposed to spend all of Saturday block-walking, which meant knocking on strangers' doors to ask who they were voting for and remind them about Janet. But a lot of kids didn't even show up for the block-walk, and out of those of us who did, most bailed within an hour.

I could hardly blame them. It was properly fall now and starting to get chilly. Saturday was windy and drizzly—a type of weather that does not even crack Janet's top ten. Most of the doors we knocked on never got answered, either because people weren't home or because they wouldn't open the door when they weren't expecting guests. We managed to connect with a few people, and they were generally nice to us—one even brought us towels so we could dry off from the rain. But by the end of the day I had a blister on my heel and a nagging suspicion that I wouldn't have achieved any less had I just stayed home under a blanket.

I reminded myself that every vote mattered and every person we spoke to brought us one step closer to winning. But the number of registered voters was so huge that it was hard to imagine how knocking on thirty doors and talking to four people could make enough of a difference to matter. If only there were some way to personally go to *all* of their houses and make sure they *all* opened their doors.

On Sunday, the skies were clear, but I just couldn't face any more block-walking. Instead, My Friend Daniel and I stood outside of Lions, Tigers, and Bears with clipboards, and we talked to customers as they went in and out of the store. We were still bothering people, but at least we didn't have to bother them in their homes.

Lions, Tigers, and Bears was the big costume shop in town, so they did a brisk business every October. I liked to make my costumes from scratch so I'd look different from everybody else, but I usually got a wig or face paint or some other material from this store. Shopping there in the days immediately before Halloween was impossible; the line was always out the door. But Halloween was still a week and a half away, so today Lions, Tigers, and Bears was bustling but not *too* crowded.

"Do you know who you're planning to support for mayor?" I asked a man who was walking out wearing a pig mask.

He glanced at our "Janet for Mayor" sign and said, "Not that girl. I'm definitely going with the other candidate."

"Why?" My Friend Daniel started to whine, but I clapped a hand over his mouth, and the man took off his pig mask and walked away.

"Daniel," I said, "there are a bazillion prospective voters to talk to. We can't waste our time on people who already have their minds made up. You know this."

"Yeah," Daniel said, "but his mind was dumb."

"Okay, well, I don't think telling him that was going to help Janet win, do you?"

Daniel sulked until the next person came along. "Do

you know who you're supporting for mayor?" he asked the man pushing a baby carriage toward us.

The guy shook his head and said, "Not yet."

"Can I talk to *him*?" Daniel asked me.

I rolled my eyes. "*Yes.*"

"Sometimes I'm not allowed to talk to people," Daniel told him snottily. "Anyway, here's what I like about Janet Teneman and why you should like her, too . . ."

"Do you know who you're supporting for mayor?" I asked the next woman who came my way.

"Myself," she said icily.

I looked up at the woman.

It was Lucinda Burghart.

"Are you Halloween shopping?" I asked, trying to imagine what Lucinda might dress up as.

THE WICKED WITCH OF LAWRENCEVILLE

MISS DARTH VADER

SHE WHO MUST NOT BE NAMED

"No," replied Lucinda. "I am not Halloween shopping."

"Oh."

"I'm here to talk to you," Lucinda said.

"Me?" I literally looked behind me. There were eighteen days until the election. Lucinda should be talking to her campaign staff, her donors, the voters. There was no reason why she'd want to talk to *me*.

"Yes," Lucinda said. "Come with me." She started striding briskly away. I grabbed Daniel by the wrist and chased after her. We caught up with her at the end of the block. She turned around and said, "Who is this?"

"My Friend Daniel," I said.

"I don't need to talk to Daniel," she said dismissively.

"Well, I'm not just going to follow you by *myself*," I explained. "And I'm not leaving Daniel alone back at Lions, Tigers, and Bears."

"I don't see why not," Lucinda said.

"You might be a kidnapper," My Friend Daniel pointed out to her.

She sighed. "Fine. Daniel, you will come with us."

"*Are* you going to kidnap us?" Daniel asked, rooted to the sidewalk.

Lucinda closed her eyes briefly. "No," she said. "I am going to buy you ice cream."

CHAPTER 22

Sprinkle 'n' Scoop had all its Halloween decorations up. Disembodied plastic fingers and eyeballs decorated our table. It looked creepy, which was exactly how I felt about being here with Lucinda. My Friend Daniel was clearly immune to the ambient horror. "You're actually

really nice," he informed Lucinda as he dug into his ice cream.

Lucinda gave him a thin-lipped smile. "As are you, Daniel."

I rolled my eyes. Just because Lucinda had bought us ice cream, that didn't mean she was suddenly a good guy. I'd ordered a single scoop of Dutch chocolate. And I hadn't taken a bite yet.

"This is quite enjoyable, isn't it," Lucinda remarked. But I don't think she meant it, because she said it in the same tone of voice as Grandma when she once described my collage of hair trimmings as "interesting."

"Now, what grade are you children in?" Lucinda asked.

"Seventh," Daniel told her, his mouth full of ice cream.

DANIEL'S ICE CREAM

Cookies 'N' Cream

Frozen Banana

Rocky Road

What kind of monster puts raisins in ice cream?

Is that a sandwich buried under here?

I don't even know what this is

"And what's your favorite thing to do at school?" Lucinda asked.

"Social studies is my best subject," Daniel said. "And I'm on the soccer team now."

"An athlete!" Lucinda beamed at him. "Just like me. Keep your head in the game, and someday you could make it to the Olympics. It really is possible—and I should know." She paused, waiting for one of us to be like, *Oh, really? How do you know that? What is your Olympic-related experience? Do tell!*

"Daniel's on the Yellow Team," I told her. "He's not going to the Olympics."

"What do *you* like about school?" Lucinda asked me.

"Art," I answered, looking her in the eye.

"Well, then, you're in luck," Lucinda said, "because I have a proposition for you. I'd like to keep arts education funding for Lawrenceville schools. In fact, I'd like to double the budget. How does that sound?"

"So you just . . . changed your mind?" I asked, hardly daring to believe it.

"I listened," Lucinda explained. "That's part of my job as a representative: to listen to what the people want. At the debate, I heard the voters say that they value arts education and they want to continue to fund it. My job is to give the people I represent what they want."

"Really?" I asked. I finally took a bite of my ice cream. It was delicious.

"See? I told you she was nice," Daniel said.

"Whatever you may think of me, I'm not out to get you," Lucinda told me. "I'm not motivated by a desire to make life worse for anyone."

"Then why threaten to get rid of arts education in the

first place?" I asked, confused. This all seemed too good to be true. Was this a trick? Or had we . . . won?

"Every politician's goal should be to make his or her city better for its citizens and taxpayers," Lucinda explained. "I am confident that the way to do that here is to lower taxes and to keep the government out of things that shouldn't be its job in the first place. I thought that eliminating arts education would be a good way to help accomplish that. But your advocacy has convinced me otherwise."

"Wow," I said. I couldn't believe it. Our campaign had actually made a difference! We'd changed people's minds, and we were going to change people's lives.

"Would you like that?" Lucinda asked. "If I am elected mayor, would you like me to leave your art classes alone?"

"Yes, please!" I said.

"Wonderful," Lucinda said. "Consider it done." She took a last sip of her raspberry lime rickey, dabbed at her lips with her napkin, and then said, "There's just one small thing you can do for me in exchange for my generosity."

"What is it?" I asked.

"Stop working on Janet's campaign."

My eyes widened. "What? Why?"

"Because," Lucinda said patiently, "we are making a political compromise. An alliance, if you will. I'm offering you something that you want, and in exchange, you can give me something that I want.

"You—all your little friends, those hordes of children I see everywhere with 'Janet for Mayor' signs and flyers and whatnot—you will all cease involvement with Janet's campaign. Go back to focusing on your schoolwork and test preparation, as you should have been doing all along. Go back to your art projects, since you feel like they are so important. Leave the election to the grown-ups."

Daniel nodded, like this made sense. "I *would* like more time for soccer practice," he agreed. "And then you would just take care of the art thing?" Lucinda gave her assent, and Daniel grinned at me and said, "Perfect!"

I stared at Lucinda, my brain whirring. "Hey," I said, suddenly realizing why she'd brought us to Sprinkle 'n' Scoop. "You're scared of us."

"Excuse me?" Lucinda laughed.

"You actually think we might win."

"No," Lucinda said. "I'm confident that I will win. But I also believe in being prepared, and I do not leave things up to chance. Now, what do you say to my offer?"

"We say yes," My Friend Daniel said, licking his spoon.

"Daniel!"

"What? It's the solution to everything. We get to keep art class, *and* we get to stop working so hard. Win-win."

It sort of seemed like he had a point when he put it like that. "But what about Janet?" I asked.

"You won't need Janet," Lucinda replied. "You'll have me."

They both looked at me. I felt sick. I pushed away the remains of my melted ice cream and said, "I need to think about it."

Lucinda pursed her lips together and nodded. "What

a focused young woman you are," she said, making it sound like a criticism. She handed me a business card.

"Here's my email address. If I don't hear from you within forty-eight hours, then this deal is no longer on the table." She stood up, pushed in her chair, then looked at me.

"Just know this," she said. "I will win no matter what you do. And if you choose to continue this absurd, selfish little campaign against me, then *when* I win, I will destroy every last scrap of arts programming that your school has. It will all be gone. Poof! And you will have only yourself to blame."

"Why are you so mean?" I asked, staring up at her.

"Mean?" Lucinda laughed. "I'm not mean. I'm presenting you with a choice. You wanted responsibility? Well, I'm giving it to you. Your future and the fate of all your friends rests in your hands. Now it's up to you to choose wisely."

CHAPTER 23

There weren't that many people working at Jordan's the next day. Maybe the ineffective block-walking had scared them off. Michaela was at a computer, entering contact information for new Janet supporters. Deke was calling voters whom we still hadn't managed to reach, but mostly he was getting sent straight to voicemail. My Friend Daniel was playing a video game. Otherwise it was calm. Depressingly calm. And I couldn't figure out what to do about Lucinda's offer.

Molly and Polly and Holly were there, too, but they weren't doing anything useful. They were singing along with the soundtrack from *Grease* and making poodle skirts for their Halloween costumes.

"We should start at my house," Molly was saying. "My neighborhood has the best candy."

"But my house is the best for getting ready," Polly disagreed. "My bathroom has a huge mirror. Plus, I don't need your sister bugging us the entire time we're there."

"How long could it possibly take you to get ready?" I spoke up. "You're all doing the exact same costume. Just do it once and then copy it." They all ignored me, but I was too worried to be ignored. "The election is coming up right after Halloween," I reminded them.

"So what?" said Molly.

Holly gave me a Holly Look.

"So, do you really think we have time for trick-or-treating?" I said. "Shouldn't we be working on the campaign? You know Lucinda won't be taking a break for Halloween."

"No way am I giving up *Halloween* for another night of making phone calls and holding signs," Molly said. "You're crazy."

Maybe I *was* crazy. Crazy for believing that Janet could win. It was time to face the facts. My classmates' initial excitement about the campaign had waned and been replaced by Halloween, sports practice, play rehearsals, homework, and tests. People were sick of knocking on strangers' doors and making phone calls and getting no replies. Despite all of our best efforts, Janet was still polling ten points behind Lucinda, and I didn't know where we were going to find the votes we needed to make up the difference. *I will win no matter what you do,* Lucinda had told me yesterday. And I had the horrible suspicion that she might be right.

In which case, wouldn't it be far more strategic to give up now and make sure we got to keep art class?

"Fine," I said sarcastically. "Go trick-or-treat. Have fun."

"Ugh, Maddie, why do you always act like you're better than us?" Polly asked me.

"What?" I shook my head. "No, I don't."

"Yeah, you do," Polly said wearily. "You think our Halloween costumes are boring and dumb because they all look the same. Well, we *like* looking the same. So what if you're going to do something different and wow-nobody's-ever-thought-of-that-before for your Halloween costume? Why is that any better than what we're doing?

"And now you're acting like caring about Halloween at all is silly, because it's not the thing *you* care about right now. Just because *you* don't like a thing, Maddie, doesn't mean that everyone who likes it is pathetic."

My mouth was agape. "I've never called you pathetic."

"You don't have to say it. We're not stupid. We can tell when you're judging us. You're not subtle about it."

"I'm having a rough day, okay?" I protested. "What if we lose? I can't just hang out and plan a trick-or-treating route when all I can think about is how we might lose!"

"Are you *always* having a rough day?" Polly asked. "Because you *always* treat everyone like your stuff matters more than their stuff."

"That isn't fair."

Polly shrugged and went back to her poodle skirt. "If you say so."

"And anyway," I yelled, "why should *you* care what I think? Everyone already loves you. You tell them to do something, and they do it. Actually, you don't even have to *tell* them—they just *see* you doing something, and they want to copy you. Everyone wants to be friends with you and be in your dumb plays and hear all about your dumb Beyoncé concerts. Why isn't that enough for you? Why do you need *me* to be obsessed with you, too?"

"Firstly," Polly said, "that's not true. Secondly, I don't want you to be 'obsessed' with me. I'm just asking you not to be outright rude to me and my friends. We're doing a ton of work for this campaign, just like you. So stop acting like whatever we do isn't good enough for you."

This wasn't fair! At all! *I* wasn't the bad guy here—Molly and Polly and Holly were. *They* were the mean, popular clique, and I was the artist who cared about downtrodden outsiders. *They* were the judgmental ones—they told me I was weird all the time and laughed at me for doing things 'the wrong way.' So how dare they act like any of this was my fault?

"You know what?" I said. "This campaign is over."

"What?" Michaela asked. Now even she, Deke, and Daniel were looking at me.

"It's over," I repeated. "We fought a good fight, but it's not worth it anymore. It's time to face the facts: Lucinda is the real politician here, and she's going to win. She was *always* going to win. She has more money, more experience, more connections—there's nothing we have that she can't beat."

"So you're *quitting?*" Polly asked, wrinkling her nose.

"You all clearly want to. So why don't you just go ahead? You won't have to put up with me and my 'judgment' anymore. Because I'm going home. And you should, too."

And as soon as I got home, I would tell Lucinda the news: I was taking her deal.

CHAPTER 24

I stormed out of Jordan's, my head down, hands in fists, and almost ran into the garbage man. "Hey, kid," he said. He'd become a lot friendlier since I'd told him Janet wanted to increase the sanitation department's budget and hire more people to work there.

"Hey," I muttered, not looking at him. I knew I was being rude, but my eyes felt tense and hot, and I was worried that if I said more than a few words, I'd start crying. "Sorry," I said. "I don't really feel like talking."

"Who feels like talking?" the garbage man asked. "I don't feel like talking. Well, maybe I do, but I certainly don't have time to talk. Do you have any *idea* how many stops I still have to hit today?"

I shook my head, averted my eyes, and tried to find a way around him.

"But you know what helps?" he said to me.

"What?" I mumbled.

"Knowing that it's not forever. Knowing that when Janet gets elected, she'll make this better."

I finally looked up at him. Tears threatened to spill out of my eyes, but fortunately, the garbage collector didn't seem to notice.

"It's not just me," he said. "Every garbage collector in this town is fed up with how we're being treated. We're all supporting Janet. We even got pins made. See?"

I stared at the pin. I didn't really care how many people worked for the sanitation department. It had nothing to do with me. I wasn't a garbage collector, I probably never would be, and the farthest I'd ever carried a trash bag was from my front door to the curb.

But this issue mattered to the garbage collectors just as much as art class mattered to me. They wanted a leader who would try to fix their problems just as much as I wanted a leader who would try to fix mine.

Maybe I could get Lucinda to add this to our deal. I'd

tell her that we'd stop campaigning for Janet so long as she promised to give us arts education funding *and* sanitation department funding. She would probably agree to that. Right?

But then I started thinking about all the other people who'd asked Janet for so many other things over the course of this campaign. How Molly wanted more street-lights so she wouldn't be scared walking in the evening, and Isabelle wanted high-speed internet, and Dylan's sister wanted to be able to afford community college, and Theo's dad wanted to be able to afford to buy a house. Everybody wanted something, and they were all depending on Janet to help them get it.

And who was I to say that art class mattered more than the rest of it?

Daniel had told me that I only thought about issues that directly affected me. Polly had told me that I judged other people for caring about things I thought were dumb and worthless. And I had told them both that they were wrong, because I didn't want those things to be true.

But what if they were?

I could have a guarantee that my own life would get better if I started supporting Lucinda.

But I had a chance at making *lots* of lives better if I stayed with Janet.

I turned around and marched back into Jordan's Hot House. Everyone looked up at me warily, like they thought I was going to yell at them again.

"Daniel," I said, and he paused his game. "I'm sorry that I acted like your soccer team doesn't matter. Dahlina"—she crossed her arms—"I'm sorry that I acted like your play and your Halloween costumes are dumb. Adrianne, I'm sorry that I've been calling you Molly like I don't even care what your name is. I've been rude to all of you, and I'm going to try to do better.

"But you've laughed at me and called me names, and even though I try to act like I don't care what anyone thinks of me, I can't help but care. When people tell you all the time that you're a weirdo, it makes you feel like one. When no one wants to hang out with you, it makes you feel like you're not worth hanging out with. I'm sorry I've treated you badly. I think I was just trying to get revenge for the way you've treated me."

And then something happened that I never would have expected: Holly spoke up.

"I'm sorry, too," she said. "You're different, but that's

not really a bad thing. In fact, maybe it's a *good* thing, because only someone who's different would have put together a campaign like this. If you weren't different, Maddie, then nobody at all would be trying to stop Lucinda."

"Whoa," I said, staring at her. "You talk?"

She gave me a Holly Look.

"Oh, that was me being judgy, wasn't it?" I realized. Everyone in the room nodded. "Sorry about that," I said to Holly. "And thanks."

"Look, we've spent a ton of time working together," Polly/Dahlina told me, "and I've realized that maybe you're not as weird as you seemed before I got to know you. Or, like, maybe you *are* that weird—but it's a good weird."

Makes hilarious weird jokes!

Thinks up brilliant weird ideas!

OOD WEIRD MADDIE!

Wears gorgeous weird clothes!

Draws awesome weird pictures!

"I'll take good weird," I replied. "And now there's something I need to do . . ."

I pulled Lucinda's business card out of my pocket and quickly sent her a message. Here's what it said:

I didn't care if she ever wrote me back.

My Friend Daniel clapped his hands. "Will you come to my bar mitzvah?!" he hollered at the room at large.

Everyone turned to look at him.

"What?" Molly/Adrianne asked.

"You know, now that we're all friends," Daniel explained.

Holly gave him a Holly Look.

"Hey, Daniel?" I said. "Let's come back to that. Right now, we have a campaign to run."

"I thought you said we shouldn't even bother because there's no way we can win," Dahlina pointed out. "You said there's nothing we have that Lucinda doesn't."

"Well," I said, picking up her poodle skirt, "you made me think of one thing."

CHAPTER 25

A woman in a witch's hat opened the door to 414 Noble Street.

"Trick or treat!" we shouted.

"Happy Halloween!" she replied. "My, look at your darling costumes! Now you, of course, are a soccer player," she said to Daniel.

"I'm a *Red Team* soccer player," he informed her.

She smiled and looked puzzled. "And you are," she said to me, "a . . ."

"Superwoman banana ballerina fairy," I explained.

"Ah, of course. Well, you are both very spooky indeed," the woman told us, and she dropped mini 3 Musketeers bars into each of our pumpkins.

MADDIE THE SUPERWOMAN BANANA BALLERINA FAIRY!

"Thank you!" I said. "We also wanted to remind you that Election Day is on Tuesday. Do you have plans to vote?"

"I . . . yes?" The woman looked thoroughly confused by the change in conversational direction.

"Great!" Daniel said. "This is going to be a very tight race, so your vote is incredibly meaningful. Will you consider supporting Janet Teneman for mayor?"

I pulled a glossy "Janet for Mayor" flyer out of my pumpkin and put it in the woman's hands. "Janet is the only candidate who is going to expand public services, repair what's broken in this city, and—most importantly for us—give us the kind of well-rounded public school education that we need."

"Can we count on your vote on Tuesday?" My Friend Daniel asked.

Well... sure! You can count on me.

Daniel and I high-fived as we walked back down the driveway to the street. "That's ten," he said.

"Well, they didn't all say they'd support Janet," I reminded him. "Four of them said they would, one of them said he couldn't vote but he'd tell his dad, and the others said they would think about it."

Daniel made a face at me. "I meant that's ten candy bars."

"Sure," I agreed. "But *also* ten possible votes for Janet."

I looked up the street. It was crowded with ghosts and vampires, Harry Potters and Elsas, Mickeys and Minnies and Minions. They were all carrying bags of candy. And they were all carrying postcards for Janet.

It's hard to ring strangers' doorbells. It's hard to strike up a conversation with someone you don't know. It's hard to get people to open their doors for you.

But you know when all of that's *not* hard? Halloween.

On Halloween, everyone is home and ready to open their door with friendly smiles. And if they're not? Then they just turn off their lights, so you don't even have to waste any time trying! It's a perfect system for getting candy . . . and for getting votes.

And getting kids to agree to participate? That was

easy, too. We were all going to spend hours walking around town and ringing doorbells anyway. Might as well canvas for Janet while we were at it.

So we didn't just get the kids who were actively involved in the campaign to help. We got kids from all the different clubs and cliques at school, from all different grades. We even got the elementary school kids involved—everyone with younger brothers and sisters gave them flyers, and then the younger brothers and sisters distributed the flyers among their friends. There were hundreds of us out on the streets tonight, and we all had the same goals: get candy and help Janet.

"Should we go up Maple or stay on Noble?" I asked Daniel when we reached the next intersection.

A little boy with a puffy coat over his princess dress overheard me and offered his opinion.

"Yuck," Daniel and I both said. "We'll stick with Noble."

The kid gave us a salute and then ran off in pursuit of more non-raisin treats.

By eight o'clock, we'd picked up so much candy our arms ached, and we'd handed out all of our Janet flyers. We headed to Jordan's to see how everyone else had done.

Jordan's was even more crowded and noisy than usual, and when we first walked in, I felt overwhelmed. Most years when we were done trick-or-treating, My Friend Daniel and I would return to his house, and we'd trade and categorize candy until my parents came to get me. I wouldn't describe it as *calm*, since we were always hyped up on sugar, but at least it was just the two of us. This was like . . . a party.

"Do you have any Milky Ways?" Michaela shouted as soon as she saw us. She was dressed up as a lady ghost.

"No way," I replied, holding my pumpkin closer. I don't trade chocolate things. It's just a rule.

I will trade you literally anything for a Milky Way!

"Would you trade me *two* things for a Milky Way?" Daniel asked her.

"Depends on which two." They dumped out their candy and started inspecting each other's wares.

"Maddie, catch!"

I looked up just before a Starburst hit me in the head. I unwrapped it, stuck it in my mouth, and grinned at Dahlina, who had thrown it to me. "Thanks," I said. The Starburst was pink, which was pretty generous of her. Everyone knows that pink Starbursts are one of the best non-chocolate foods out there. "How'd it go?"

"So good," she said.

"We hit fifty-two houses!" said Adrianne. "See, I told you guys my neighborhood has the best candy." She fluffed her poodle skirt proudly.

"And I convinced two undecided voters to vote for Janet," Holly announced.

"How did you do that?" I asked. "Like, with your voice?"

She gave me a Holly Look.

Dahlina grabbed me and pulled me onto a beanbag chair with her.

"You're right," Adrianne said. "No kids would want to go trick-or-treating for her."

"She wouldn't care if they did," I said. "She has a lot of money and a professional campaign staff and a fancy campaign office, so what would she want with trick-or-treaters? She doesn't believe that kids can do anything important."

Dahlina grinned. "Well, then she's not going to believe what we did tonight."

I grinned right back at her, and I gave her a Hershey's Kiss. Like I said, I don't trade chocolate. But sometimes I give it away.

My mom came to pick me up at nine. "Bye, Maddie!" everyone shouted as I left. "Happy Halloween! See you tomorrow!"

I had to take off my banana suit so I could fit into the car. Once I was finally buckled in, Mom asked, "So you had a good time tonight?"

I watched Jordan's through the window, all its lights on, all the costumed campaign workers making so much noise that I could still hear them even out here. "Yeah," I said as she started up the car. "I really did."

CHAPTER 26

THE LAWRENCEVILLE GAZETTE

THE *LAWRENCEVILLE GAZETTE* ENDORSES JANET TENEMAN FOR MAYOR

A surprisingly contentious election season draws to a close on Tuesday, when voters will at last head to the polls to cast their ballots for Lucina Burghart or Janet Teneman.

Both are excellent candidates, each of whom would bring very different strengths to the role. Burghart offers decades of experience in city government and a demonstrated commitment to making budgets as lean as possible. Teneman brings fresh energy, new ideas, and vision for the city's growth. Depending on your priorities, either candidate could be a solid pick. After much deliberation, however, our editorial board has given its endorsement to Janet Teneman.

Teneman has proven herself naturally able to connect with the public. She demonstrates the true spirit of a civil servant, seeking the mayorship in order to help her fellow citizens rather than to grab power for herself. And the public has responded to her concern for them with a groundswell of support. In debates and town halls, Teneman has shown herself to be well-intentioned, if not as well-informed as her competitor. Becoming the mayor would be a steep learning curve for her, but we believe that she is more than up to the challenge.

The polls are open on Tuesday from 7:00 a.m. to 7:00 p.m. Visit the city's website for information on polling locations and absentee ballots.

Tuesday was the big day.

Election Day.

The polls didn't open until seven in the morning,

but I woke up at five and couldn't fall back asleep. All that work over the past few months—all the rallies and debates and flyers and postcards and phone calls—came down to today.

And if people *didn't* turn out to vote for Janet today, then it wouldn't matter how many doors we'd knocked on or how much money we'd raised. All of that would be for nothing if people didn't actually get in the voting booth and select her name.

I lay in bed, knotting my sheets around my fingers and wondering how I'd gotten into such an intense competition when I didn't even *like* competition. I'd submitted a comic to *Fishsticks* last year, and that was competitive in a way, but the editors of *Fishsticks* could accept as many comics as they wanted. I'd once entered a drawing into an art contest, but I knew that if I didn't win, there was still a chance I could get second place or an honorable mention or *something*.

A political race wasn't like that. There was one winner, and they got to be mayor for the next four years, and everyone else got nothing at all.

For maybe the first time ever, I was downstairs and ready for school before my parents even got out of bed.

I heard my mom's watch alarm go off, her cue to come down to the kitchen and start the tea kettle.

"Ah, yes, of course." Mom sat down next to me and placed her hand on mine. "Sweetie, I'm so proud of all the work you've put into Janet's campaign."

"Thank you," I said, snuggling into her.

"And I just want you to know that no matter what happens out there today, she'll always be your babysitter."

I looked up at my mother. "You know that's not true, right? Because if she gets elected, then she'll be the mayor, not my babysitter. And also I'm practically old enough not to need a sitter at all."

"Right," Mom agreed after a pause, and I got the sneaking suspicion that none of this had ever occurred to her before. "I just meant . . . in our hearts, she will always be your babysitter."

"Okay," I said dubiously.

"Okay," Mom said.

Dad drove me to school early, because I was too jumpy to stay at home and do nothing. I knew Janet was already out there, going from one polling place to the next to introduce herself to voters as they came through, and I felt like I needed to be out there, too.

Lawrenceville Middle School's gym was one of the city's polling sites, so rather than just drop me off like usual, Dad parked and came in with me. There were signs all over the school building that said "Vote here" in various languages.

We were among the first people there. The PTA was still setting up the bake sale, which made me wish we hadn't gotten here quite so early. The banana chocolate chip muffins looked really good, but we couldn't buy them yet. Dad gave his name and address to the poll worker, and she handed him a ballot.

"The first time I ever voted, it was for President John F. Kennedy," Dad told me. "He was a great man. One of the greatest. He died too young."

"He died before you were born," I pointed out.

Dad looked at me.

"I learned that in social studies," I said.

"The first time I voted, it was for someone with just as much courage and character as JFK," Dad said.

"Who?" I asked.

"A great man. Great politician. I don't remember his name."

"Did he win or lose?" I asked.

"Oh, he won," Dad said as we took the ballot into the voting booth. "He won in a landslide."

"Good for him," I said. The voting booth wasn't totally isolated, but it was private enough that nobody other than us could see who Dad marked on his ballot.

"I think I already do," I said. For the past ten weeks, I'd been following the news, learning about the issues, talking to other citizens about what they believed, and trying to turn my beliefs into reality. That was democracy. I was already living it.

But there was also a part of me that felt sad and left out when I saw my dad choose Janet's name in the mayor category. Because for all that I had done, I couldn't do that one last thing. I could urge hundreds or thousands of people's hands toward Janet's name, and in that regard my influence was limitless. But I could not select her name myself—I couldn't select *anything* directly—and in that regard I was powerless.

I had done everything, and now that we were actually here at the polls, I could do nothing. Nothing but hope that what I'd done already would prove to be enough.

The poll worker handed my dad a sticker that said "I Voted," and he stuck it to his coat. "Do you want one too, honey?" the poll worker asked me.

I knew she was being nice, but that made me feel left out, too. "No, thanks," I said. "I *didn't* vote."

We got a few steps away, and then I had an idea. "Actually—" I turned back toward her. "I'll take one of those stickers after all."

And after applying a little bit of artistic flair to it, I wore it with pride.

Dad gave me a kiss and headed to work, and I headed upstairs to social studies. Dahlina, Adrianne, and Holly came in soon after, all of them staring at their phones. "There are no updates," Dahlina was grumbling. "This website is supposed to give us minute-by-minute updates about voter turnout, but it's been stuck at fifty-six for ages now. Only fifty-six people have voted? Where is everyone?"

"There still aren't any exit polls," Adrianne complained.

Holly gave a Holly Look, though it was directed at her phone, not at me.

"You know the polls have just barely opened," I reminded them. "We won't know anything for a while."

"Oh!" Dahlina gasped.

"What?" I leapt from my chair and ran around to see over her shoulder.

"More voters turned out in the first hour of polling today than in the first hour of Election Day last year!"

"That's awesome!" My Friend Daniel said, arriving and tossing his backpack on the floor. "Better voter turn out favors *us*, because that means more first-time voters, and first-time voters are more likely to support someone who's young and new, like them."

"*Maybe*," Adrianne said, "but maybe it just means that Lucinda has done a really good job of energizing *her* base and this high voter turnout is all because of kid haters flocking to the polls."

"Why isn't there more information?" Dahlina snapped, refreshing the web page once again. "How old are these first-time voters? Who are they? Why is no one telling us anything?"

"Guys!" I said.

They all looked at me.

"Nobody knows anything yet," I said. "Okay? Everyone's just guessing. We don't know anything because *nobody* knows anything, because there's nothing to know yet."

"Okay," Adrianne agreed, but she definitely wasn't listening to me, because a minute later she added, "Hey, this reporter just tweeted that she thinks Janet's chance of winning is almost equal to Lucinda's!"

The rest of the school day went the same way. None of us could pay any attention. Who could focus on algebra knowing that while we were stuck in here solving for *x*, vote after vote was being cast all over the city? I'd never seen so many cell phones get confiscated during class, as kids kept pulling them out to sneak just one look at the news. And in the hallways between classes? Forget it.

"How are you feeling?" Mr. Xian asked when I showed up to art class.

I shook my head and blew out a long breath. "Nervous," I said. "Sad. Proud. Overwhelmed." I shrugged. "Everything."

Mr. Xian nodded like that made sense, even though I myself couldn't begin to make sense of my own tangle of emotions. "You know what I do when I feel everything?" he said.

"You draw?" I guessed.

He grinned. "Now, how did you know what I was going to say?"

So I spent the next forty-five minutes with my headphones on, sitting quietly on the floor and drawing. It didn't change anything in the world. But it did make me feel better.

"Maddie," Mr. Xian stopped me as I was on my way out of class. "Thank you for trying to save my job."

"You're welcome," I said.

"I'm serious," he told me. "There are so many people who cry and complain when something happens that they don't like. And then after they're done crying and complaining, they just go along with it. You saw something you didn't like, and you took action to change it. And you never quit."

I thought about getting ice cream with Lucinda, and I blushed. "There were some times when I nearly quit," I admitted.

"But you didn't," Mr. Xian reminded me. "And you won't. Even if Janet loses, you'll find other ways to fight for the arts."

"It'll be easier if she wins," I pointed out.

"Yup," he agreed. "But if she doesn't, then you'll do it the hard way."

I gave him a smile. "Thanks, Mr. Xian."

"Now, go to class," he said, "before Ms. Castro yells at me for making you late again. Whatever happens, I'll see you back here tomorrow."

"Tomorrow," I repeated. Tomorrow everything would be different.

MY EVERYTHING DRAWING

CHAPTER 27

After school, we divided up. We had kids stationed at every polling location around town, holding "Janet for Mayor" signs so people could find us and ask any last questions as they headed inside, and of course Janet was still trying to visit all the polls before they closed. You're not allowed to campaign for a specific candidate within a hundred feet of a polling site, so we measured out the distance and then stood as close as possible.

Lucinda had people holding signs for her at each polling place, too. I tried to ignore them.

"Thanks for voting!" the woman with the Lucinda sign called to everyone as they left. "Let me know if you have any questions!" she greeted everyone who approached. "Do you want any gum?" she asked me.

I shook my head. No way was I taking poison-laced gum from the enemy.

She smiled at me and popped a square of gum into her own mouth. Okay, maybe it wasn't poisonous. Still, I didn't want anything from her.

"What grade are you in?" she asked me.

"Seventh," I said. I wished she would quit acting so friendly.

"Oh, seventh grade was the worst," she said. I looked

at her. "Sorry," she said. "If you love seventh grade, that's great! I wasn't trying to ruin it for you. I just recall that it was hard for me, that's all."

"Why?" I asked, interested despite myself.

She made a face. "English isn't my first language, so I didn't talk much, because I was terrified that the other kids would make fun of the way I spoke. One of my teachers was really horrible, and he *did* make fun of my accent."

"No!" I said. "A *teacher*?"

"Not a good one," she said. She handed a "Lucinda for Mayor" flyer to an arriving voter and brightly said, "Vote for Lucinda!"

I studied her. She seemed kind. Honest. If she weren't out here campaigning for Lucinda, she seemed like someone I could even like.

"Why are you supporting Lucinda?" I asked. *You don't seem like a jerk*, I added silently.

"She has a good plan for bringing more businesses into Lawrenceville," the woman answered. "I think everyone can agree that there's a serious unemployment problem here. There are far more people who want to work than there are jobs, and I believe that Lucinda is the most likely to fix that."

"Janet wants to bring more jobs here, too," I pointed out.

"I know that," she acknowledged. "And Janet seems great. I can see why you support her. It just seems to me that Lucinda's plan is more likely to succeed."

"Yeah, but she's . . ." I didn't want to say it, but it sort of had to be said. "Not very nice."

The woman said, "The thing about politics is that it's not good guys versus bad guys. Everyone pretty much wants the same things: a safe and affordable lifestyle, growth opportunities for our kids, justice, and freedom. We just don't all agree on what the best way is to get those things." A new family walked by, and the woman smiled at them and called out, "Thanks for voting!"

I didn't know what to say to any of that. I'd always thought of politics as kind of like this:

RIGHT VS. WRONG

Which meant that everybody who didn't support Janet was selfish or stupid or evil. But this woman didn't seem to be any of those things. She was just ... different.

When Deke came to relieve me, I didn't exactly know how to say goodbye to Lucinda's sign-holder. I felt like I should wish her good luck, but I didn't *actually* want her to have good luck, because that would mean bad luck for me. She must have seen my confusion, because she smiled at me and said, "Thanks for participating in democracy. I hope we get a government that we can both feel good about."

"Thanks," I said. "I hope that, too."

I passed my sign to Deke and was about to leave, and then guess who showed up?

Lucinda.

Of course it made sense that she was spending Election Day visiting all the polling sites, just like Janet. So I guess I wasn't surprised to see her. But I wasn't happy about it, either.

"Maddie Polansky," she said coolly.

"Lucinda Burghart," I said back.

She narrowed her eyes, studying me like this was her first time truly seeing me. "Who *are* you?" she asked at last.

I almost felt bad for her. Obviously she had some made-up idea in her head about who twelve-year-olds were and what we could do. But the truth was, she didn't know anything.

"I," I told her, "am the campaign manager." And I walked away.

By the time I got to Jordan's, there were only two hours left until the polls closed. As soon as I walked in the door, Michaela handed me a list of names and phone numbers. "These are all Janet supporters," she told me. "They're all people who we coded as ones and twos when we were doing voter identification. Once you get through these names, come to me, and I'll give you more."

I found some space at a table and started making my phone calls.

"I still need to get to the polls," said the first guy I spoke with. "I got stuck at work."

"You only have two hours left," I told him.

"This is the third time you people have called me today," complained the next person I reached.

"Well, we're going to keep calling you until you vote," I replied. "So you should go do it, and then we can stop bothering you."

I hung up. I called the next voter. I hung up. I called the next voter.

"Come on, people!" Michaela yelled. "Pick up the pace!"

More kids arrived, and Michaela handed out more contacts.

"I really hate talking on the phone," Adrianne whined. "It makes me nervous."

"None of us like it, Adrianne," Dahlina said. "That's not why we're doing it."

"I already voted," said the next person I spoke with.

"I'm just leaving the polls now," said the one after that.

"Everyone in this household voted for Janet!" said someone else.

"Thank you," I told each of them. "Remind all your friends and neighbors. Make sure everyone you know votes before it's too late!"

All the phone conversations started to bleed into one. My ear started to ache, and my fingers grew stiff from dialing. I wanted to stop, but I didn't. Because this was it. This was the final push. And then Michaela said:

"Okay, that's it. The polls are closed."

We all set down our phones, and for a moment, the room, which had been vibrating with conversation for hours, fell silent. We had turned out every voter we could. And now it was too late to do anything more. Now it was out of our hands. All we could do was wait.

CHAPTER 28

Janet arrived at Jordan's soon after the polls closed. She'd spent the day meeting as many voters in person as she could. And now she was here with us, her campaign staff, to watch the results come in.

Dahlina put the news on the big-screen TV, and we all filled up bowls from the candy machines and settled in to watch the results.

"Lawrenceville is divided into thirty-two precincts," the news reporter was saying. "We'll report results from each precinct as they come in, but remember that it takes some longer to report than others. Our first precinct reporting this evening is the twenty-fourth."

The TV showed a map of the town with the twenty-fourth precinct highlighted, and Isabelle proudly announced, "That's where I live."

"The twenty-fourth precinct reports five hundred and eighty-five ballots cast for Lucinda Burghart and one hundred and thirty-one for Janet Teneman," said the newscaster.

The mood in the room sank immediately. Janet's face drooped, and a few kids let out outraged gasps.

"No offense," Dahlina said to Isabelle, "but your neighborhood stinks."

But the next precinct they announced was Dahlina's, and that one went for Lucinda, too—437 to 294.

"*Your* neighborhood stinks," Isabelle told Dahlina.

"This whole *town* stinks," said Lucas.

"We're still at only 6 percent reporting," I reminded everyone. "Anything could happen. The next 94 percent of votes could all be for Janet."

But that wasn't what happened. The next precinct came in, and it was 514 to 291 in favor of Lucinda. So far, Janet had picked up more than 700 votes, which wasn't *bad*. Given that ten weeks ago nobody knew who she was and eight weeks ago she was just "that girl who cheated in high school," it was impressive that more than 700 people trusted her enough to go out and vote for her.

But Lucinda already had more than double that many votes, and they just kept coming in. Every time Janet edged up, Lucinda did, too.

"She's cheating!" My Friend Daniel squawked.

"How is she cheating?" I asked.

"Because . . . she's winning!" Daniel said.

"*Winning* is not the same as *cheating*," I pointed out.

"Yeah, but we worked a lot harder than she did! And Janet's a better candidate! It's not fair!"

I shoved away my bowl of candy. I wasn't hungry.

When Lucinda passed 2,000 votes and Janet was still at 1,200, Janet stood up to address the room. "I know that this evening isn't going the way we hoped," she said. "And it's okay to feel upset about that. We all worked really, really hard. I am so proud of every one of you.

"When we started this race, I knew we were fighting an uphill battle. I didn't know if we could win, but I knew that we could call attention to the issues that mattered, fight strong, and fight fair, and that's exactly what we've done.

"I'm sorry if I've let you down by not being a good enough candidate. But I want to make sure you know that none of you let me down. You did the exact opposite. You have given me so much hope for the future."

I wished I could pause time right then. I could see my life unrolling before me like a road with no turnoffs. Tonight, Janet would lose. Tomorrow, all my classmates would go back to not spending time with me, not relying on me, not including me. Next year, art class would go away. I would always remember that there had been this brief period of time when I was important and valuable, when people wanted to hear what I thought. A brief period of time when I could do things right. But that time was almost over.

Enjoy it right now, I told myself, *because it's never coming back.*

Then Holly cried, "Look!"

She was pointing at the big screen behind Janet. The seventh precinct had just come in, and it was reporting 650 votes for Janet and only 358 for Lucinda.

Lucinda's lead had been cut down to 500 votes.

She was still winning. But not by much.

When the next precinct came in with 610 for Janet and 347 for Lucinda, the room started buzzing. And when the one after that gave Janet 599 votes and Lucinda 269, there was a collective gasp.

By the time half the precincts were reporting, Janet's total vote count had surpassed Lucinda's.

"What's happening? What's happening?" My Friend Daniel asked, frantically shoveling candy from my bowl into his mouth.

"I don't know," I told him.

Janet's eyes were so wide I thought they might pop out of her head. I crawled through the rest of the kids to stand next to her and hold her hand.

When the next precinct reported, Janet's total was 150 votes higher than Lucinda's. With the one after that, it was back down to only fifty more. Then it was back up to 130 more. Then 200. Then 240.

"With all thirty-two precincts reporting," the newscaster said, "the final vote counts are 12,474 for Janet Teneman and 12,101 for Lucinda Burghart."

The room erupted.

"Does that mean we win?"

"Is it over? Can I look?"

"I can't hear what they're saying!"

Janet's phone began to ring. I let go of her hand so she could fumble it out of her pocket.

"Everyone shut up!" Dahlina hollered. "Janet has a call!"

We all shut up.

"What was that? What happened?" we all cried.

Janet looked dazed as she slid her phone back into her pocket. "That was Lucinda Burghart," she said. "She was calling to concede." And Janet started to laugh. "We won, guys. We won! I'm going to be mayor!"

CHAPTER 29

We celebrated late into the night.

It was over. We had won.

I couldn't wrap my head around it.

Tomorrow I would go to school, and I'd see Mr. Xian, and he would still have a job. Mrs. Cheng would, too. Lucas would still have band, and Chloe would still have *Fishsticks*, and Dahlina could star in every single play from now until high school graduation.

And I would still have art.

And that was all I'd ever wanted. But somehow, it didn't feel like enough anymore.

I'd always felt like I needed only one place where I belonged, and that was art class. It didn't matter that in every other part of my life I was awkward and confused and wrong, because when I was doing art, I was just right.

But for ten weeks now, I'd had this *other* place where I belonged. It was here, on Janet's campaign.

I was so grateful that we'd won—I honestly was—and I didn't want to have any bad feelings at all. Not tonight, when we had so much to celebrate. But I sort of wished that instead of winning the election, the campaign could have just gone on forever.

My Friend Daniel felt the exact opposite. "I am so happy that this election is over!" he hollered. "Now I can finally stop spending so much time on it!"

"I can actually focus on *The Lion King*," Dahlina said. "We only have four weeks until the show goes up, and I'm not even off book yet because I've been so busy with the campaign!"

"I'll finally have time to start my a cappella quartet!" said Deke.

Everyone had lives they were eager to restart. Everyone except me. We'd been a team for a while. And now everyone would go their separate ways, and I would go nowhere.

I never would have imagined this before, but it turned out I really liked being part of a team.

So I cleared my throat and did something I'd never done before. I said, "Can I help?"

Here's what I thought was going to happen:

But here's what *actually* happened:

"Okay," I said, and I started to smile. "I'd like that."

"They'll all be lucky to have you," Janet told me. "Just don't get *too* busy with all those extracurricular activities, okay? I still need you!"

"For what?" I asked. "The campaign's over, Janet. You're going to be in charge now. You don't need any more help!"

"Are you kidding?" she said. "People who are in charge need the *most* help! You're going to be one of my chief advisors, Maddie. I mean, assuming you're up for it. I couldn't have done any of this without you, and I don't want to start now!"

I gave her a big grin. "I'm up for it," I said.

The campaign was over, it was true. But somehow, I felt like we were just beginning.

EPILOGUE

"How do I look?" Dad asked as we got out of the car at the Lansdowne Hotel. He fussed with his tie while Mom gave the car keys to the valet.

"Very handsome," Mom said, giving him a kiss. It was January now, two and a half months after the election, and it was dark and snowing lightly. I could see my breath in the air.

"You know," Dad said to me, "this is the very same suit that I was wearing the day I asked your mom to marry me."

"Really?" I asked.

"You weren't wearing a suit when you asked me to marry you," Mom said drily as she ushered us into the hotel lobby. I was wearing shoes with a little bit of a heel, so I had to climb the stairs carefully and hold up the hem of my dress so I wouldn't trip.

"Is that so?" Dad looked puzzled. "Huh. I could've sworn I was wearing this." He patted the pockets as though searching for proof.

The receptionist greeted us with a smile. "I'm going to guess from your outfits that you're here for the mayor's inaugural ball," she said.

"We are," I confirmed.

"Tickets?" she said. Mom reached for her fanny pack to get them out, then remembered that for once she wasn't wearing a fanny pack because I'd told her that it didn't go with her floor length gown.

The receptionist checked us off her list. There was a man in a tuxedo standing in front of the doors to the ballroom, and I thought maybe he would tell me I couldn't come in, like that guard at the debate. But instead he opened the doors for us, and I stepped into Janet's party.

My Friend Daniel and his parents were already there, and they came up to us and started chatting. "I want my bar mitzvah party to be exactly like this," Daniel told me. "Except with a magician. Janet should've hired a magician."

Daniel was the only person at the party not dressed in a fancy outfit. He was wearing a T-shirt and his Yellow Team bandana instead. He basically hadn't taken it off since they had finally won a match. Michaela and I had gone to cheer them on.

I think he was glad we went to his match to support him. That's what friends do, after all.

And tonight, *everybody* was here to support Janet at her inaugural ball. I saw Mr. Xian and Mr. Okereke and the principal and Mayor Peñate and the debate moderator and the editor of the *Lawrenceville Gazette* and Janet's parents.

The only person who hadn't come was Lucinda Burghart, even though Janet had invited her. Janet said she wanted to be the mayor for *all* of Lawrenceville, not just the people who'd voted for her, especially because the race had been so close. And that meant working with Lucinda to make sure that her supporters felt heard and represented, too. But apparently Lucinda didn't want to be here tonight. I thought she was a sore loser. She should be used to losing by now, really. After all, she had lost the Olympics.

I spied the rest of the kids over by the food table, loading up on cheese cubes and mini brownies. "Can I go hang out with my friends?" I asked my parents, and they followed me over to the refreshments.

"We are all so fancy!" Dahlina shrieked when she saw me.

And we *did* all look nice. But the real star of the show was Janet. She was glowing. When she got up on stage, every eye in the room followed her.

The cheers were deafening. I clapped so hard my hands hurt.

"Thank *you!*" Janet said. "I am so happy to be here tonight. Did you all notice that it's snowing out? How amazing is that? I cannot imagine better weather for the day I take office! I hope that every day that I'm mayor, Lawrenceville gets weather that's as perfect as today's."

After a bit more of that, Janet finally moved away from the weather and started talking about her plans for when she was mayor and thanking people—the voters, her parents, all the kids who trick-or-treated for her.

"I wouldn't be here at all if it weren't for one person in particular," Janet told the crowd of hundreds. "And that's Maddie Polansky. Maddie, are you out there? Can you wave?"

"She's right here!" Dahlina, Adrianne, and Holly shouted. They all pointed at me as I blushed bright red and gave a little wave. Everyone clapped.

"If you ever doubt that one kid can make a difference," Janet said, "talk to Maddie, and she'll prove you wrong."

I couldn't stop smiling.

"You know what?" Mom said, like she was realizing this for the very first time. "I'm proud of you."

"Me?" I asked.

"Yes, you. You really did all of this. You didn't just read about it and think about it and talk about it; you went out there and *did* it. None of us would be here right now if it weren't for you, Maddie."

"Well," I said, "other people helped."

"I wonder if I could ever do something like this," Mom mused.

I grinned. "I bet you could," I told her. "If you want, I could even teach you."

"You know what just occurred to me?" Dad said, "When Janet starts being mayor tomorrow, she probably won't have much time to babysit for you anymore."

"That *just* occurred to you?" I asked in disbelief.

A man I sort of recognized came up to me then, and he stuck out his hand for me to shake.

Congratulations on your big win, Maddie. My name is Chris Prince, and I'm a political organizer.

I know who you are.

"How do you feel?" Chris asked me, gesturing around the room.

"So proud," I said.

"There's nothing like your first win," Chris said. "Every win is special—every race is special, and every candidate is special, whether they win or lose. They all matter. But the first one is like nothing else."

"My *first* win?" I repeated. "What makes you think there will be a second?" I still wanted to be a professional cartoonist, after all. And maybe design graphic T-shirts, too. I don't know. I'm twelve. There's still time for me to do anything.

Chris grinned at me. "For those of us who care about what happens in the world around us, our work is never done. Remember, there's an election every year. And there are campaigns for civic causes that never stop. You won this race, but there are plenty more that need your energy and dedication. Tonight, you bask in your victory. Tomorrow, you change the world. What do you think?"

I looked around the ballroom—at my parents, my friends, my teachers, my ex-babysitter and now mayor.

At the balloons and the chandeliers and the cake. At the joy and the anticipation for all the good we could do. And I smiled.

"All right," I said. "Tomorrow, let's change the world."

AUTHOR'S NOTE

Like Maddie, I got involved in my first political campaign when I was twelve years old. I volunteered on the campaign for a politician named David Cohen, who was running to be mayor of Newton, Massachusetts. He won, and while I definitely didn't play anywhere near as major a role in his campaign as Maddie did in Janet's, I loved being part of it and feeling like my small actions were contributing to a greater cause I believed in.

What I learned then, and wanted to get across with Maddie's story, is that government affects basically everything about how all of us lead our lives. It affects whether our parks are maintained, whether our drinking water is clean, whether our stoplights function, whether our neighborhoods are safe. Every day, we interact with government in so many ways that we don't even think about. Journalist Christopher Hooks phrased it like this in an essay for the website Medium: "That's what politics is—the way we distribute pain. It's not a sport or a fraternity or a game. It's how we determine who gets medication and who dies young, who learns in a class of twenty kids and who learns in a class of thirty, whose school has a counselor that's trained to look for signs of sexual abuse and whose doesn't."

Because politics affects all of us almost all of the time, we should all understand the basics of how it works. As Mr. Valdez explains to Maddie, American democracy depends on a system of checks and balances. There are three branches of government:

The *legislative* branch writes and votes on laws. On the national level, this is the House of Representatives and the Senate, which together form the Congress. In Lawrenceville, this is the city council.

The *judicial* branch interprets how those laws are applied and decides whether those laws are constitutional. This branch is made up of judges, and the highest-ranking part is the Supreme Court.

The *executive* branch administers and enforces those laws. On the national level, the leader of this branch is the president. On the state level, it's the governor. In Lawrenceville, it's the mayor.

Each of these branches keeps one another in check,

so no one person or part of the government can get too much power. When all power is consolidated in one person, it's called a *dictatorship*.

The ultimate check on governmental power is the people. Citizens of a democracy get to vote for their governmental representatives, and if we don't like what they're doing, we can vote them out, protest their actions, or even run against them. Members of the government know that they could lose their jobs if enough people don't approve of what they're doing, so they have an incentive to listen to the people and try to give them what they want. Basically, we as a country are the employers of the lawmakers, and if they're doing a bad job, we can fire them.

The media play a big role in helping the people exercise our governmental oversight. The internet, newspapers, magazines, radio, and TV keep us informed about what our elected officials are doing. That's how we find out if our representatives are doing something we don't like. It's also how we find out if they *are* doing things that we like, which is how we know to support them in their campaigns.

If you want to make a difference in politics like Maddie and her friends, here are some things you can do:

COMMUNICATE WITH YOUR ELECTED OFFICIALS. Tell them what matters to you and what actions you want them to take. Like Maddie, you can go to a town hall, or you can show up at their offices to tell them in person. Or you can call, write letters, or send email.

JOIN ADVOCACY GROUPS. If there's a particular issue you care about—the environment, smoking, gun control, school uniforms, or anything else—there is most likely an advocacy group that is working to make a difference in that realm, and they are usually looking for volunteers to help with their efforts. One way to find advocacy groups is through Charity Navigator (www.charitynavigator .org/). Social networks like Facebook and Meetup (www .meetup.com/find/movements/) can show you groups that are near you. And of course, asking other people who are politically involved to recommend groups is the best way to get personalized ideas.

FORM A CLUB AT SCHOOL. If you care about an issue that doesn't already have a group at your school, start one yourself! Talk to a faculty member about starting a new student organization, invite friends to join, and use school-approved media (school newspapers, bulletin boards, assemblies, etc.) to spread the news about what you're working on.

TALK TO OTHER PEOPLE. Studies show that you're most likely to read a specific book or watch a specific movie if your friends recommend it to you. The same is true with politics. The number-one way to get other people to care about an issue that is important to you is to talk to them about it. This can mean talking one-on-one with friends, and it can also mean things like writing letters to the editor of the newspaper to reach a wider audience.

VOLUNTEER FOR A VOTING RIGHTS NONPROFIT. Non partisan groups like Rock the Vote (www.rockthevote .org/), When We All Vote (www.whenweallvote.org/), and the League of Women Voters (www.lwv.org/) work year-round to register voters and promote civic engagement. They need volunteers to help spread the message that people can (and should!) get involved in politics.

VOLUNTEER FOR A POLITICAL CANDIDATE. Even though presidential (and most mayoral) elections are held only every four years, every single fall brings a new election where other important offices are filled. Look at who's on the ballot for the next election—you can find lists at websites like Vote411 (www.vote411.org/)—find out which candidates best represent your views, and sign up to volunteer. Like Maddie and her friends, you can do voter ID or get out the vote calls, block-walk, write postcards, hold signs, gather signatures, or all sorts of other things. You don't need to do anything you're not comfortable with—there are tons of different volunteer opportunities, so whatever your skills and interests are, there should be something you can do to help a campaign.

The government has an impact on pretty much everything, but all of *us* have an impact on that government. Now, my question for you is: what sort of impact are you going to have?

ACKNOWLEDGMENTS

Sometimes a book can change your life, and one that changed mine was Judy K. Morris's *The Kid Who Ran for Principal*. I first read that book when I was eight years old, and it is long out of print, but it has had a lifelong impact on me and on my storytelling.

I can't close this book without a huge thank-you to my parents. Had you not, despite my protests, insisted on listening to NPR on the car radio every morning and every evening, I can't imagine that I would have written Maddie's story. Thank you for taking me to political protests before I was old enough to remember them, for subscribing me to kids' newspapers even though I only read the human-interest stories, and for driving me to and from campaign headquarters when other kids were going to soccer practice. Thank you for all your years of political activism and engagement and for trying to give me a better world to grow up in. You are my supporters and my role models. I love you endlessly.

Thanks to my editor, Maggie Lehrman, and my agent, Stephen Barbara, for your storytelling wisdom and for seeing the potential in Maddie's story. Thanks to the teams at Abrams and Inkwell for all their work to get this book into readers' hands, especially Emily Daluga, Marie Oishi, Marcie Lawrence, Kim Lauber, Nicole Schaefer, Hallie Patterson, Jenny Choy, Patricia McNamara O'Neill, and Andrew Smith.

Thanks to Brian Pennington, Rebecca Serle, and all the rest of my friends who supported me as I was writing this book.

Thanks to the news media outlets who strive to keep us informed about our government and give us the data and stories we need to make responsible decisions. Thanks to the teachers and librarians bringing civic education to their students all across the country. And thanks to all the principled, wise, ambitious politicians I have volunteered for and their campaign staffs, who inspired this story.

ABOUT THE AUTHOR

Leila Sales attended political rallies when she was a baby, started a petition against her third-grade language arts textbook, volunteered for her first mayoral campaign when she was twelve, and as a teenager competed in debate competitions all over the world. Since then, she has built a career as a critically acclaimed author of many middle-grade and young adult novels, including *Once Was a Time* and *This Song Will Save Your Life*. She is also the editor of award-winning and bestselling books for children of all ages. She still cares about politics. Learn more at LeilaSales.com, or follow her @LeilaSalesBooks.

ABOUT THE ILLUSTRATOR

Kim Balacuit is an illustrator and designer who studied animation and illustration at Montclair State University. She lives in Rutherford, New Jersey, and is fond of animals, banana bread, and long road trips.